MW01505747

BY

ÉLIETTE ABÉCASSIS

A Couple

TRANSLATED FROM THE FRENCH
BY JOHANNA McCALMONT

This is a work of fiction. Names, characters, places, and incidents
are from the author's imagination or are used fictitiously.

W1-Media, Inc.
Grand Books
Stamford, CT, USA

Visit our website at www.arctis-books.com

1 3 5 7 9 8 6 4 2

The Library of Congress Control Number: 2025930054
ISBN 978-1-64690-049-7
eBook ISBN 978-1-64690-050-3

English translation copyright © Johanna McCalmont, 2025

Excerpt on page 13 translated by A. S. Kline, 2021.
From Letter VII
Used with permission by Poetry in Translation

"L'Été indien", Joe Dassin, lyrics by Toto Cutugno, Vito Pallavicini,
Pasquale Losito and Sam Ward, adapted by Claude Lemesle
and Pierre Delano., CBS Disques, 1975.

"Histoire d'un amour", Dalida, lyrics by Carlos Almarán, adapted
by Francis Blanche, in Gondolier, Disques Bar-clay, 1958.

Printed in Germany

BY

ÉLIETTE ABÉCASSIS

A Couple

To Ethan, who inspired this story.

1.

Paris, May 2022

"May I?"

The old man indicates the space on the bench next to the woman who is sitting upright, a serious air about her, one hand on her cane as she stares into the distance.

She turns round to look at him. He is handsome, his salt and pepper hair, thick for his age, swept back on his head. His smile lights up his thin, angular face, which is speckled with small age spots. His eyes are a piercing blue—the left one serious and earnest, the right one happy.

"Of course, please do."

With a nod in reply, he notices her high cheekbones, red-rouged lips, fine, parchment-like skin, wrinkled hands, and visible veins. She smiles kindly at him. Her hair is perfectly set, like she has just left the salon, and she is wearing light summer pants and a beige wool twin set. She straightens her curved back, correcting her posture. Delicate, slim, and quivering, she looks like a reed that might bend in the wind.

They are in the Jardin du Luxembourg, a place she likes to come, always to the same spot, on the right as you look at the pond, beside the rows of green chairs.

She looks straight ahead again, focused. Her face, marked by the passing of time, crisscrossed by deep lines, settles back into a serious expression like she is waiting for something or someone. She left home alone, walked along Rue Lhomond, down Rue d'Ulm to the Pantheon, then took the grand Rue Soufflot to get to the Jardin du Luxembourg. She sat down on her favorite bench to rest at the pond where children sail remote-controlled boats. This is where she cat-naps, reflects, and slips back into her memories. When she was younger, she used to walk down the long path to the Sorbonne where she was studying, to the feminist meetings in the cafés in the Latin Quarter, and to the jazz clubs in Saint-Germain at night.

She looks up and observes the man who has sat down beside her. He's dressed elegantly, with a V-neck sweater over a white shirt and beige chinos, bright, understated colors for a spring morning when the sky is clear and the days are starting to get longer.

Paris is coming to life ahead of the *Libération* festivities to commemorate the end of the Second World War on May 8, 1945. Many Parisians have already deserted the city for the holiday. She likes how the city feels empty, reminding her of those summers when the streets were silent, subdued by the heat. That was a long time ago, when seasons were still seasons, when they hadn't become blurred.

Sitting there beside each other, stiff, moving wearily, seemingly lost in another world, smiles frozen on their lips, they try to be present, but life moves at a slower pace for those who no can longer see or hear as well as they once could—a sign that reality is slowly slipping away, along with life.

He turns to her and smiles with sadness and sorrow. She looks at him, slightly lost. Why is his left eye black? His heart condition makes life very difficult for him. He slipped on the rug in the lounge and lay there for hours with no one around to help. He developed sores and has slowed down now. His arthritis makes walking hard, but sometimes he forgets and dashes down the corridor like he's in a hurry—that's how he tripped. He fell on his side, bumped his head on the corner of the coffee table, and ended up with the black eye that makes him look like a pirate or bullfighter. Since then, he has had a domestic helper, but he doesn't like other people touching his body that has become so unwieldy, heavy, and weak despite his solid frame and swimmer's physique.

His hearing isn't what it was; the batteries in his hearing aid wear out too quickly. Sometimes, it's a while before anyone changes them for him, so he gets caught off guard by loud noises. It's like the volume is too high, and he is surrounded by a deafening din, so in the end, he prefers silence. Unless he's watching television, fascinated by the plethora of new channels that offer him a window onto the world, a world now beyond his reach, apart from through his memories, ones he likes to recall from the time he helped build the world and make it more inhabitable with the projects he worked on. A school, a town hall, quite a few houses, apartment blocks, countless renovations. And the ones that will never see the light of day: hotels in Iceland or South America, villas made entirely of glass, ridiculous towers erected with a dash of a pencil on his architect's drawing board.

She listens carefully, her hearing not what it once was either, but out of vanity, she refuses to get a hearing aid. Architect, that's a nice profession. How does he come up with his buildings? Does he have visions? Where does his inspiration come from? Does he like Bauhaus?

Her cell phone rings, and she pauses. Slowly, she gets it out of her small red leather purse, along with her glasses so she can see the button to answer the call. "Where are you? I was worried. I called you a couple of times, but you didn't pick up. You know you're not supposed to go out on your own."

She sighs and looks at the gardens. A gentle breeze rustles the majestic, exotic trees and the enormous sequoias that cover them like a canopy of centennial shade. A ray of sunlight pierces the foliage. The air is sweet; it is almost like being in the countryside. She hangs up and carefully returns the phone and her glasses to her purse.

"It was my son," she explains. "He calls ten times a day. He used to come here as a child. He could stay for hours, playing with just a few stones. Sometimes, he'd put them in his mouth, and one day, he even choked on one. My husband saved him with the Heimlich maneuver."

Her husband—this was where she had told him she was pregnant with their second child. He hadn't exactly jumped for joy at the news. And over there, near the pond, they had kissed for the first time. And this bench was where they had met one May afternoon. That's why she likes coming here.

She runs her hand through her hair to straighten it, still looking at him solemnly.

"It's so sad," she says.

"What is?" he asks.

"I miss my life. My old life."

"Which life?"

"The one I had with my husband and children. It feels like there's a permanent vacuum. It feels unfair," she says.

"That's not what feels wrong: it's living against the flow that feels wrong. Not being of your time."

She doesn't reply. He wonders if she heard him. He repeats what he just said louder; she jumps and turns toward him.

"In my head, I'm twenty years old," she murmurs.

"Don't tell me you're not twenty?" he jokes, smiling.

"Almost ninety! And you?" she asks.

"Same as you?"

"We're old, aren't we?"

"Not as old as when we weren't . . ."

All of a sudden, a phone rings: Joe Dassin's *Indian Summer*. This time, he reaches for his cell phone at the bottom of his pocket. But he doesn't get it in time, and the song stops.

"That will be my daughter," he says. "I think she's waiting for me."

He suddenly looks at her, worried.

"May I?"

He dares to take her hand gently. He holds it for a few seconds before bringing it to his lips and closes his eyes for an instant.

"I once loved a woman too," he says. "As soon as I met her, I proposed. I didn't know her. I didn't know where she lived, so I wrote her a letter . . ."

His hands start to shake, and trembling, he brings a battered, old envelope out of his small bag, gray and perforated, and pulls a yellowed sheet of paper out of it, folded in four, covered in narrow, slanted writing. He gives it to her, and she takes it, puzzled.

Then he leans on the bench to get up, almost falls, and says goodbye with a nod.

"*Adieu Madame*," he says. "It was a pleasure to meet you."

Then he leaves slowly, uncertain of his step.

She watches him as he walks down the long path to the entrance.

"See you again soon," she murmurs, tears in her eyes.

2.

Port-des-Barques, August 2018

Sitting on the small garden patio beside the sea, Jules re-reads the letter he found in the drawer of the desk he shares with his wife, the letter he wrote after they met in May 1955. The thin paper has resisted the passing of time, his tight, slightly slanted handwriting still legible. It's like the first time he's ever seen it. He smiles and is surprised at the emotions that well up again, so many years later, and also at how presumptuous he had been. He studies it carefully, searching for obvious signs of the effect of time, notices how the ink is fading, the lines and curves, guesses a few words that have almost become illegible, strokes the yellowed paper, and holds it against the light with his marked, worn hands. This letter hasn't aged, he thinks, even though he struggles to hold it because of the pain spreading through him, and that's when morbid thoughts overwhelm him. His limbs feel heavy, and a multitude of minor aches and pains restrict his freedom. Alice takes care of him; he relies on her day after day. She is the one who counts out his pills and gives them to him each morning. He doesn't even know what he's taking, neither the names of the drugs nor the doses. She arranges his doctor's appointments and visits to the physical therapist, the hairdresser, the ophthalmologist, the gastroenterologist, and friends and family, too; she organizes every aspect of his daily life. Since his retirement, he has delegated his entire life to her. She has become his mother, his sister, his friend, his doctor, his nurse, his caregiver, his therapist, his cook, and his personal secretary.

Their house in Charente-Maritime is a modern home with white walls and a large bay window that looks out over the ocean. They love to watch the colors change, from morning to evening, in good weather or stormy weather, changing from the darkest grays to the brightest of blues. They retired here after Jules had the house built to his plans, just as he had pictured it: clean lines and full of light. They had rented out their apartment in Paris, bought a small pied-à-terre in the Latin Quarter, brought their things, their books, their clothes, and their habits to take up residence in the middle of nowhere, in this far-flung corner they had discovered on one of their trips to the country. Even though there aren't many people around and the area can feel as if it's desolate in winter, they like it. They go grocery shopping, on trips to the Ile de Ré, long walks along the shore, to the western point, and to the Phare des Baleines lighthouse, where the fresh air from the open ocean hits you in the face. Jules loves this corner of the world.

Alice has settled into this life, too. She enjoys the sunsets tinged with hues of red, yellow, and purple when the sky is set alight at the end of the day, like a ball of fire sinking into the ocean. It's in this unlikely, almost dream-like place that she has started to collect family photographs and documents in order to draw the family tree. She spends hours contemplating and painting this natural beauty that only reveals itself at dusk. Now that she has time, she carries out research, using place names, marital statuses, marriage certificates, family documents, and old photographs, along with the genealogy websites that are flourishing online. Like a detective, she investigates her ancestors and has traced her family tree back five generations. She is the daughter of Alexandre Edelman, a litera-ture professor, and Clara Aron, a violinist. Her parents are the children of Moïse and Colette Edelman and Étienne and Judith Aron, and the grandchildren of Richard and Alice Edelman, Isidore and Simone Dreyfus of Phalsbourg in Lorraine. Among her ancestors, she discovers a textile merchant for the army during the time of the Napoleonic wars, a tycoon or "financier" as they were called back then, a confectioner from Lorraine, a cattle seller in Poland, and even a government minister, teacher, and general inspector who helped found the École Normale Supérieure college in Fontenay-aux-Roses to train women teachers.

Why does she want to reconstruct the past? Jules wonders. *What good will it serve? My memory isn't what it used to be. I want to slow down time, this feeling that everything is wiped out, and I'd like to bring the dead back to life through my ancestors. Do you know your family's history? With the mar-riages and births, I'm trying to identify the crucial moments when fates are decided; out of all the possible configurations of our lives until then, the way they sometimes develop unbeknownst to us. Sometimes, I feel that particular sense of weariness that comes with old age, so I remember my youth. I manage to chase away the fear that paralyzes me, that constant feeling of running after my own existence, and find that vague sense of happiness when time stops. And in this new period of my life, I feel a need to become immortal through transmission, something that cannot exist without a sense of the past. With genealogy, I ask myself fundamental questions about an existence that is constructed and deconstructed. I prefer solitude; I like being in a shack at the end of the world. That's where I feel most free because I no longer depend on anything or anyone, not on this strange world whose values, lives, and traditions I have studied since I retired. But to really exist—I don't know if I'm still able to. For that, you would have to live, and I no longer think I have the strength to do so. I told you I would help you. But I feel uncomfortable with all these dead. Who amongst them are still alive? Am I still alive in your eyes? Do you remember the sofa bed in our small apartment in Rue Mouffetard, where we laughed, cried, and lived on love and freshwater? I used to cuddle up beside you and whisper in your ear how beautiful you were. Stunning with your straight dark hair that fell over your shoulders, your doe eyes, and your sweet flowery vanilla smell.*

As Alice watches the horizon turn purple every day, the heavens clothed in their best finery as though offering a palette to a heavenly painter, she allows herself to be amazed and astonished, two childlike qualities that Alice hasn't lost despite her age, and she is finally reunited with her childhood memories once more. Her face, tanned by the sun that has sprinkled it with age spots, relaxes, her expression softens, and she feels happy. With her small mouth, a beauty spot above her lip, her brown eyes, slim nose, thick eyebrows beneath a crown of dark hair, cropped short with bangs, she moves slowly, like a shadow, leaving a wake of that sweet perfume she has always worn. She holds her straw hat tight around her face to protect her hair from the wind and spends hours contemplating the horizon and the boats sailing across it, lost in her thoughts and smiling at her memories. It is always the same ones that come to mind: those few days in Naples and on Capri during her honeymoon, a trip to Venice, the two-room apartment in Rue Mouffetard, the children playing in the garden, like layered snapshots, or photos you look back at, images in a kaleidoscope that make up the film of her life.

In the summer, she goes swimming when it's high tide, heading out from the shore,

like she's trying to cross the Atlantic while Jules watches her, worried, his hands shading his eyes. He can stand staring after her for an hour. Each time, he imagines the worst. He can't help it. All of a sudden, he loses sight of her and starts to panic. His heart stops beating until he sees her again. He waves to her to come back, but she moves further away, alone, like she wants to prove her strength and her freedom. That's when she experiences that exhilarating feeling of being somewhere between heaven and earth, of being weightless. Each time she comes back, he welcomes her warmly, relieved, like she has just escaped serious danger. Yet he tries not to show her that he was afraid, terribly afraid.

A few times a year, their children or grandchildren join them in Port-des-Barques. Since his divorce, their dear son Alexandre has come here with his daughters every August. Thanks to social media, he found his young love again, a woman he met at university. Their daughter Émilie comes to visit during Christmas and Easter. She moved to London with her husband and three children and lives in Soho, where her parents visit her less and less often. Jules didn't want to travel anymore, so Alice ended up going alone and then no longer going at all. It's too far, too difficult, and too unsettling for her now, and she prefers to stay at home.

Clara and Léa, their granddaughters, are only interested in the fairytale sunsets along the coast and creating stories, with their long, straight hair, fake eyelashes, pink lipliner, and perfectly white smiles after years of visits to the orthodontist, making V for victory signs with their pink nails.

They have sunk into the sofa in the lounge, glued to their cell phones, headphones on their ears. Jules' laptop is on the table beside her. He only turns it on occasionally to catch up with emails and read the papers online, including the one about modern architecture he set up with a colleague. He uses Skype to talk to his son, who has called him every day since he took over the business and is now successfully working on the site for the multimedia library Jules never managed to finish himself. There is a pretty Art Deco lamp on the desk in the lounge, with a pewter base and a white glass shade—a gift from Jules to Alice that he found at a flea market after a very long hunt and brought home triumphantly one Mother's Day. Alice has lit it every evening ever since and likes the soft light it casts over the room.

Clara logs back on to a new dating app to continue a chat she started the previous evening.

What do you do?

I travel . . . I'm an airline pilot.

Wow! How do you keep it up? It must be crazy. Long or short haul?

Both. I'm leaving for Berlin soon, for example.

Divorced father, I see?

Yes, I've got one child and a double life that suits me perfectly. Every other weekend, I'm a doting father, and during the week, I'm single. I like the combination. It's perfect! You get kids and fun.

"Who are you writing to?" asks Alice, reading over her granddaughter's shoulder curiously.

"A stranger."

"Aren't you a bit young for that?"

"It's just for fun, Grandma. I'm not really going to meet him."

Did you enjoy Berlin?

I loved it. I went to bars after work.

"Berlin," Alice murmurs. "Did you know I went there to see the Berlin Wall come down in 1989?"

"What did you do, Grandma?"

And what about you, what do you do?

"I was reporting for a newspaper. It was a time when everything changed. The end of one world. The entire Communist Bloc was collapsing! Two years later, the USSR no longer existed."

I'm a journalist.

"And was Grandpa with you?"

"No. He was working."

Which paper?

"Which paper did you work for Grandma?"

"The *Nouvel économiste.*"

The Nouvel économiste.

Does that still exist?

"And did Grandpa travel too?"

"At one point, yes. Grandpa often traveled outside Paris for his projects."

"Grandma," Léa interrupts, "what age were you when you met Grandpa?"

"Eighteen."

"That's young!"

"We were more traditional. He proposed to me before he even kissed me."

"And as soon as I'd met you," adds Jules.

"But you saw May '68, didn't you Grandma?" Clara says. "That must have been crazy!"

"Yes. We were activists. Grandpa was a Trotskyist; I was a feminist."

Can we do a video call, Clara?

"Did you and Grandpa call for the sexual revolution?"

"We were . . . like everyone. Well, I was for it. I took part in the November 1971 demo, the big march to break the chains of slavery. We demanded the freedom of abortion and the right to contraception. The crowd went into a church during a wedding to try to stop it. We chanted, 'Marriage is a fool's trap!' Three years later, the magistrate Simone Veil passed the law legalizing abortion."

Alice tells her granddaughters how she covered the event for a newspaper backed by Jean-Paul Sartre that had just been set up by former Maoists and whose name echoed the Resistance, *Libération*. She still remembered Simone Veil's speech. "No woman resorts to abortion lightheartedly. One only has to listen to them." And her arguments: injustice and inequality that affect women from modest backgrounds. In the parliamentary chamber, people were agitated, the atmosphere was tense, and everyone was talking over each other. She faced a gentlemen's club of suits and ties, only a few women dotted about the 490 members of parliament. Everyone held their breath as the law was adopted, a victory for the French women's liberation movement, the MLF.

Alice looks at her granddaughters. With their grayish-blue eyes, thin mouths, and high cheekbones, they look like their father. Since their parents' divorce, they have been subject to a joint custody agreement, a double punishment for them, one week with their father, one week with their mother, packing their cases like poor little souls, giving them two homes, cut in two, between two birthdays, two dinners, two sets of parents—resulting in four parents, eight grandparents and an uncountable number of uncles, aunts, and cousins—not to mention notebooks, homework, friends, ideas, dreams, desires, their future and their past, and even who they are. Seeing their grandparents still together after such a long time is impressive and reassuring for them.

What are your hobbies and your passions in life?

"How did you and Grandpa meet?" the young girl asks, looking at her grandmother.

Alice and Jules are sitting on the sofa, in their favorite spot, where they settle down to read magazines or books.

"It's a long story," Alice says.

"A story that starts with a letter," Jules adds.

Encouraged by their granddaughters, Alice and Jules tell them how they met in May 1955 and the very special occasion that day: a marriage that was like a presage of their life together.

"Who were the happy couple?"

"It doesn't matter," Jules says.

"Yes, you remember very well," Alice says. "Why don't you want to tell them?"

"Yes, why not?" the girls ask, curious.

Because. It would take us too far back. So far back, we'd never return. So far back, we'd never get out again; we'd get lost in our memories. The story is so unlikely they'd never believe it. The story of their life is like a stratum of layers of things forgotten and left unsaid.

Had it been love at first sight? More a glance that turned into a look, attention, interest. They had talked, danced together, eaten and drank together, and gone out onto the terrace to look at the stars. As he had looked up, Alice had taken advantage of the opportunity to disappear; it had been almost midnight. Jules had tried to contact her, to find her, but he didn't know where she lived. It was long before the time of cell phones and the Internet. He had no way of contacting her and didn't have her phone number, so he wrote her a letter, such an unusual letter, so intense and so beautiful that she couldn't be anything other than moved by it. No one had ever spoken to him like that, right to his heart. But how could he post it if he didn't know her address? So he carried it everywhere until they met again, by chance or by necessity.

"Do you still have the letter, Grandma?"

"I don't know where it is . . . Do you know Jules? I can't find it anymore."

"No," he lies without batting an eyelid.

He knows very well where it is. Every day, he unfolds it and folds it up again, like a talisman, as though he doesn't want to forget when he can feel that his memory is failing and needs tangible proof of his past.

"It's the kind of letter . . ." Alice says. "The kind of letter you only receive once in a lifetime. That you read and read again. I read it again at different times of my life, you know, until I knew it by heart. It's a real letter, yet it also seems unreal. Sincere, loving, charming. Both real and imaginary. Visionary and crazy. Well, it was a message I simply couldn't resist. I'd never read anything like it. I wondered if the man who had written it was completely mad or quite simply a genius. I also thought he was making fun of me. That it was some sort of joke. Then I told myself that I couldn't let someone like that slip through my fingers. Because I had fallen in love with him, even if I didn't want to admit it, but I had fled him, thinking he wasn't for me."

"Look for it, please. I really want to read it!" says Clara.

My passion is writing. I would love to write novels. And you?

I love music.

What kind?

I'm a rap fan. Bigflo & Oli, Booba, Jul . . .

"Okay, darling. Okay."

"Tell us what you wrote, Grandpa."

But Jules doesn't reply. Lost in his daydream, he looks at his granddaughters. Talking about the past plunges him into an unfathomable nostalgia; he fights a sense of depression that has eventually engulfed him with age. He thinks back to the days when he still felt inspired and still worked, when he built houses, multimedia libraries, and auditoriums. He can feel his body giving way, his heart getting weaker, and he misses the life he used to have, his flexibility, his trips, his projects.

More and more often, he remembers his childhood in Montmartre, where he played with his friends, and how he went to school just below the Sacré-Coeur every morning, walking along Rue Feutrier at the foot of the hill. When he was young, he enjoyed roaming the hills across the city, admiring the views. He would walk around the funicular with his grandfather and take in the most beautiful panorama of Paris from the top of the steps to the Sacré-Coeur. He also liked the Buttes-Chaumont Park: steep and built on an old quarry, with its grottos and waterfalls, suspended bridge, and temple on the top of the Belvédère. The lake where the ducks and geese waded, and the view from the sloping green hills. The paved square in front of the Musée de l'Homme with its view of the Eiffel Tower and the constant whirlwind of the city. All of that energy inspired him. What was there to do now that he had nothing to gain, nothing to lose? What could he say other than to pour out his memories, ones he liked to recall with his granddaughters? What was there to tell, were it not an attempt to pass something on—but what, and to whom? And above all, what good would it do?

After lunch, Jules and Alice go for a walk along the coast while the girls stay in the house. They like to hear the beating heart of the ocean at high tide. At low tide, they can walk to the Ile Madame. They contemplate the deserted beaches with long pontoons that run out into the water, with the tiny fishermen's houses, small huts on stilts with large nets suspended over the water, where you can gaze at the horizon. They rent one for the summer to take in the fresh air in the afternoon, like they're on a boat. Peaceful moments together, talking about everything, about nothing, or remaining silent, dreaming. They have come to know each other so intimately, so deeply, that they feel a kind of harmony after a long learning process; they have discovered each other, who they are in their innermost selves. Every day, she is closer to him, and he to her, with patience, effort, perseverance, and proximity, in their small world as retirees. Marriage, life together, children—and this desire to follow their path—has made them almost inseparable over time. They have become so entwined, one with the other, that they have come to resemble each other, even physically.

"What are you thinking about?" she asks.

"Nothing."

"But you are! I can see you're worried."

"No, no . . ." he replies.

"Go on, tell me . . ."

Alice studies him.

"I'm not interested in anything anymore," Jules says.

"You're depressed."

"No. It's not depression. It's just a sense of loneliness. Yes, that's it . . . I feel lonely. As lonely as an old sea wolf! As lonely as a dog."

"And what about me?" Alice asks.

"You . . . there isn't really a you anymore."

"What?"

"You're part of me, Alice."

"You've got your children, your grandchildren."

"They don't come to visit me often. When you think about the place they once had in our lives, now they're like strangers."

"Alex works with you! You speak to him or see him every day."

"Alex doesn't need me at all. He'll do even better than me, and I'm happy for him. As for Émilie, we only see her a few times a year. I don't like her husband. He's selfish and a hypocrite."

"She feels isolated in London. Her in-laws hate her, and her mother-in-law has taken a disliking to her. She calls me in tears every day," Alice says.

"I know her tune . . . I miss you . . . I want to come back, but I can't because of Gary and the children. I feel like I've got myself caught in a trap, and it's closing in on me more every day. I don't know what to tell her; I feel responsible."

"For what?"

"Sometimes I have the feeling we weren't good enough, as parents."

"Parents are never good enough."

"And I don't know what he put into her head. When we visit, you're not allowed to eat meat, or gluten, or even vegetables unless they're organic."

"We can't do anything about it," Alice says. "You can only endure it. Observe."

"Yet if they would listen to us . . ."

"All we can do is wait until what we fear will happen happens, and then be there for them afterward, to comfort them."

"You see how alone we are."

"Your granddaughters adore you. They love listening to you and talking to you."

"But they don't come very often," Jules complains.

"Basically, you're feeling down because you're bored."

"That's true. I don't know what to do with myself anymore," he agrees.

"So I'm not enough for you?" she asks.

"You're what's keeping me alive. What would I do without you?"

"Call your friends?"

"We've both reached the age where our friends are either dead or we've lost touch. I still can't get over losing my brother. Do you understand? I don't have any family left."

Jules holds back his tears, like he always does when he talks about losing one of his relatives. Alice comforts him, reminds him of the good times he had with his brother, Sunday mornings at the football club, conversations about girls, teachers, and friends, fits of laughter, hikes in the mountains when they were sent on scout camps, those holidays that formed their bond just as much as the period after the war, their nights out as teenagers, and their preparations for their high school exams, then university exams.

"But we don't have any friends left," murmurs Jules. "I called Paul the other day, you know. I left several messages. He never replied."

"Jules," Alice says. "There's something I need to tell you."

"I'm preparing myself," Jules says without listening to her, something he does more and more often, like he hasn't heard her.

"For what?"

"I don't know. I'm on the alert. I'm watching out."

"For whom?"

"I'm starting to wonder if there is life after death."

"You know what I think about that."

"What?" he asks.

"We're made of dust, and we'll return to dust."

Jules looks at her; his blue eyes darken, and his lips quiver.

"I'm afraid sometimes," he says.

"Of what?"

"Of death. I'm afraid I'll die before you and leave you on your own. And I'm also afraid of not dying. I don't want to be left behind without you. I don't know what to do anymore or what to think. I feel like I'm losing my mind. Everything terrifies me."

"You're making me depressed, Jules. I don't know what else to say."

"And then I'm afraid they'll bury me, but I won't be dead. I'm terrified I'll wake up in a grave, alone, in the dark."

"But no," Alice says, taking his hand. "You'll be buried with your cell phone and television."

"Thanks a lot; that's much more reassuring."

"Listen, Jules . . . listen to me. I've tried to tell you this a few times, but I haven't managed to . . . Paul . . ."

"What?"

"He hasn't replied because he's not there anymore," she says.

"Where is he?" he asks, tears welling up in his eyes. Jules's grasp tightens around his wife's hand.

"What are you saying?"

"He passed away last month. His son told me. I didn't dare tell you."

"I can't breathe," Jules says. "Why did you keep it from me?"

"I was worried it would come as a shock. I was waiting for the right moment."

"I don't want to go back to the hospital."

"You only ever think about yourself, Jules. If you really want to know, I'm sad too. I'm sad that Paul died. And I miss Aunt Josette. I'm in a lot of pain, too; sometimes, I can't even get up in the morning. I'm finding it harder and harder to walk. Since my hernia, I can't digest food properly. I feel terrible after lunch, and I can't eat dinner anymore. I can't keep anything down in the evening; I feel queasy. I feel like I'm losing my mind, too. I'm starting to forget things. I'm mixing up memories. Haven't you noticed?"

"No, but you know very well that I'm forgetting everything, too."

"Sometimes I go out, and then all of a sudden, I can't remember why. It makes me panic."

"What do you want?" he asks.

"I'd like to go back to Paris."

"Turn back time . . ."

"I know where I am there; I've got my landmarks, my places. And to be closer to Alex and the girls, and Émilie, too. And I'd be happier about growing old there. There are doctors and hospitals that are easy to get to; we could get treatment, not be on our own. And you know how much I love Paris."

Jules doesn't reply, listless, contemplating the tide coming in. He's waiting for the moment when the water covers up the sand again; it could be hours before it ebbs.

"I don't only think about myself," he murmurs. "I think about you all the time, I always have, from the first time I met you. Do you remember? The wedding, that night on the terrace in the Bois de Boulogne. That night, I realized I was madly in love with you."

"You were mad, full stop. You didn't even know me. And you still don't."

"No one knows you like I do. I know everything about you. I know all your secrets. I know you betrayed me."

"You don't know with whom."

"Who was it?" he says, raising an eyebrow.

"You care? You said you'd rather not know."

"Yes, I'd like to know nonetheless."

"Why? What good would that do now?"

"Then I'll know who I'm dealing with. It's always good to know."

"So you're thinking of leaving me? At your age?" she asks.

"Of course. Why not?"

"You're terrified of being lonely. Truly alone."

"So go on . . . will you tell me who you had an affair with?" he asks.

"I fell in love," she replies.

"Yes, I know."

"Not with you. With someone else."

"Someone who wasn't me?"

"You're so arrogant! You didn't notice a thing. Yet, there was a time when I would have left everything for him."

"What do you mean *for him*? Who are you talking about?"

Alice continues, like she's in a dream. This time, she's the one who isn't listening to him, doesn't hear him.

"He couldn't leave his wife, or more precisely, he couldn't let her down. I was afraid; I was scared of getting old. I loved him—if I could have, I would have liked to have had a child with him. The day we separated, I went to hide in the bathroom to cry, and you didn't even see that I was upset. I had wanted to end everything; I had even canceled a weekend we were supposed to go away. Do you remember the weekend we were supposed to go to Naples?"

"Yes, I remember. I didn't understand why you didn't want to go anymore."

"You never understood anything. You didn't know what I was going through at that time."

"It was September 11th," Jules says. "How could I forget that? That moment when I knew that nothing would ever be the same again, and when I knew you had a lover."

Jules and Alice stare at the horizon in silence. They sit there for an hour, perhaps, each lost in their own thoughts.

"So what was it that kept us together?"

"The children," she says.

"No. We've got a very strong connection; don't tell me it was only because of the children."

And all of a sudden, as though they're afraid of losing each other, their hands touch, clasp, caress. He looks at her and thinks how he has never loved another woman. He brings her hand to his lips, missing the time when their bodies would embrace all through the night.

"Who was he?"

3.

Paris, January 2008

Jules' family and friends have come together to celebrate his
75th birthday in the loft in Montmartre that he renovated
and recently moved into with Alice. Up on the hills, amidst
the vines, the small artist's workshop at the top of a villa
near Rue Feutrier looks out over a steep lane. Jules opened
it up by taking down walls and designing a large space that
serves as a hall, lounge, and kitchen—it was sanded down,
repainted, and given structure by the wooden beams. He
enjoys strolling along the streets of his childhood, where he
and his brother Maurice used to walk to the small school
in Rue Lepic, satchels on their backs. He used to play with
his friends in the square at the top of Avenue Junot. He
knows every path, from one house to the next, hidden
stairways and lanes. He remembers the bars, the funicular, the sewing workshops, the corner shops. It all comes
back to him, and his old memories come to life again. The
paved streets with their cast iron streetlamps converge toward the basilica that lights up the hill, reminding him of
those white cakes called Merveilleux that he and his broth-

er used to admire in the windows of the bakeries. He and Maurice would play marbles while their mother cleaned the small two-room apartment where they lived. Every day, they ate their afternoon *goûter* in their grandparents' dark, narrow apartment in Rue Caulaincourt. He loved going to see them. They talked about their childhoods and the war. They had remained fearful and cautious. They were constantly stocking up and never threw anything away. They were passionate about politics. They always needed to know what was happening in the world around them. They read the newspapers every day. They needed to know everything.

After a week and a half in hospital, Jules came home tired. He has a pacemaker now. Alice takes care of him, fetches the groceries, prepares meals, and sets out his pills. She fusses about her husband like he's a child. She wakes him in the mornings and makes his breakfast, lunch, afternoon tea, and dinner. She puts him to bed, tucks him in, reassures him when he has nightmares, and takes him out to the Jardin du Luxembourg every day. There is no real conversation apart from that of a mother and child; she asks if he's hungry, if he's cold, if he hurts anywhere, or if he'd like to go for a walk. She comforts him when he cries, and he cries often. She also brushes his beautiful head of hair, a translucent halo around his smooth face, aloof, lit up by his blue eyes.

For his birthday, Alice has prepared a meal of smoked salmon, taramasalata and blinis, gherkins and potatoes—a

Russian buffet the way he likes it, washed down with vodka. Their son Alexandre has come with his wife Nelly, and their daughters Clara and Léa are playing cards at the dining room table with their grandfather and great-uncle. Jules gets a call on his cell phone: It's Émilie, who is in London for a concert. She's sorry she can't come, but she had already agreed to this event at St. Mary Magdalene church organized by an environmentalist group a long time ago. She wishes him a happy birthday, sends all her love, says she misses him, *Ciao, bye bye Papa*, then before she hangs up, she says,

"Dad . . . Gary proposed."

"Oh . . . that's a bit quick, isn't it? How long have you been courting?"

"Courting! Listen to yourself, Dad."

"I sound like someone my age. How long have you been dating?"

"That's better. But still not quite right."

"Seeing each other . . . ? Well, are you in love with him?"

"How can you know you're in love?"

"What a question!" Jules mumbles, puzzled.

"Tell me . . ."

"I think you feel it . . . It's obvious. Even if everything is against you, you don't have any doubts. It's afterward that everything gets complicated."

Jules hangs up, sad, feeling nostalgic for the little girl she once was and who he would have liked to keep close for longer. He should be happy about her news, but he'd love to dissuade her. Alexandre walks over and asks if he is okay; he can see that Jules is upset. He's not as tall as his father and feels uncomfortable about his height despite having inherited his eyes, his great hair, his thin, delicate lips, and his mother's attractive smile.

"Your sister isn't here for my birthday."

"But I'm here, Dad."

"You didn't even come to see me in hospital," Jules complains.

"I couldn't because of work; I told you that."

"Not even in the evening? And what work are you talking about? I still don't understand what you do."

"And here we go again . . . the underhanded criticism, just to bring me down as far as possible. It's no surprise that you didn't pass anything on to Émilie and me apart from a sense of guilt."

"Pardon? Do you want me to remind you of all the sacrifices I made for you both?"

"What sacrifices? All you and Mom ever lived for was yourselves. You never told us about your childhoods, your parents, your grandparents. We don't know a thing! It's as though you were just born out of nowhere. You didn't tell us about any traditions or any stories—nothing at all about our heritage. And yet you're outraged at our ignorance."

"I'm only out of the hospital, and you're attacking me."

"That's when I realized that you had failed in your role as a father."

"And you never stop, do you? It's easy to blame me for everything that goes wrong."

"I'm attacking you because I'm hurting. My psychologist has opened my eyes to a lot of things."

"Which psychologist?" Jules asks. "You're going to a psychologist?"

"Jean-Claude Bansard. Do you know him?"

"I know him. I know him very well, in fact. Isn't he a couple's psychologist? You know very well how difficult it is for us; we were born just before the war."

"And? How do you think we can build on silence?"

"How do you think we can survive without silence?"

"You know what, Dad? You've never thought about anyone but yourself. Mom's right. You were never a father. You were a friend, a big brother, a distant cousin sometimes."

"Your mother said that?"

"No, I'm saying it."

"It was supposed to be my birthday," Jules says, "not the worst day of my year. I know your criticisms and your demands, and do you want to know the truth? I don't care. So if you're not happy, all you have to do is leave Alex. You didn't need to bother coming to tell me that today."

"I'm sorry," Alexandre says, downcast. "Let's go, Nelly," he calls to his wife. "I've barely been here five minutes, and I can't take it anymore. We're leaving. Happy Birthday, Dad!"

Seeing her son leave, angry, Alice tries to make a good impression by welcoming her guests, Paul and Marie-Claude, Marc and Sophie, and a few colleagues, cousins, nephews, and nieces. There's a joyful, festive atmosphere. She drinks to forget about the tension between her husband and son, her daughter's departure, Jules' depression, and her age, which is weighing on her, this inevitable old age. Since Josette passed away, she's allowed herself a glass from time to time. When Josette was hospitalized, Alice had promised to go back and see her the next day, the day after the next, and Josette had always replied, "If you can, otherwise it doesn't matter." But Alice had never found the time—she'd had too much work, she didn't know it was important, and she didn't want to understand. It all happened so quickly. She died in her arms, and ever since, haunted by this image, Alice had struggled to accept her absence.

"Come over here, darling," Jules says when he sees her worried expression. "It's the last dance."

He sweeps her up to *Cette année-là* by Claude François, like when they were young and would go dancing at Castel. She starts to laugh, smoke, and drink; others join them— Sophie, Maurice, and the teenagers who take control of the playlist. "Relax, take it easy," Mika sings.

The music stops, and Paul takes the opportunity to say a few words. With his dark eyes, graying beard, and short hair, dressed in an Italian double-breasted suit, he is aging gracefully. In a solemn, almost serious tone, he talks about his friendship with Jules, which began as they crossed a desert in the middle of nowhere in Algeria. Jules was an officer, an ordinary soldier. They had fought together and fought the idea of fighting. And in their room at night, they had talked for hours, telling each other about their lives, their childhoods, and their war, and replied to Alice's letters.

"Together?" Alice quietly murmurs.

"I can confess," says Paul, "now that the statute of limitations has lapsed, that we wrote them together. Jules and I were devoted to each other from the very start. Without him, I wouldn't be here. He was the one who helped me, encouraged me to study at Sciences Po, and welcomed me like a brother. Without him, I would never have met my wife, Marie-Claude. It was May 1968, and we were surrounded by tear gas—that day changed my life forever."

Paul gets flustered, moved, and drinks some water. Alice takes the opportunity to bring out the cake. Jules blows out the candles, and now it's his turn to give a speech. Everyone is waiting for him, looking at him in silence while he unfolds the piece of paper with his notes.

"Since I now have the opportunity, I'd like to read you a little something I have prepared," he says. "I wrote this for you, Alice. Myself, yes, all on my own. I've always written to you, ever since we first met . . ."

Jules puts on his glasses and begins to read.

"Alice, this evening, I would like to say that without you, I would have been nothing. You are everything to me; I would do anything for you. I'm overwhelmed by what we have today and also by how I feel when I'm with you, every minute. More than ever before, I can see you fully; I know you better every day through what we have become together. Remember, I would jump into the Seine for you if you asked. I love you, darling. You are my life. What we have is extraordinary. You give me the strength I do not have and which I would find nowhere else."

Alice gives him a kiss, and the music starts again. It's the slow dance of their lives, *Été Indienne*, and they will still love each other even when love is dead. What does that mean—when love is dead?

"We've been together a long time," Jules says. "Fifty years have passed in a flash. Twists and turns like everyone else. But we've lasted. Who would have thought it when we first met?"

How have we managed it? he wonders. *With our lonely hearts, meanderings, delays, desires and weaknesses, our little dramas, and our great betrayals. How have we managed to put up with each other during the difficult times and not run away after so many years? How can we keep going as we continue to grow old? Give ourselves to each other, like each other, desire each other, betray each other and regret it, love and hate each other . . .*

Jules looks at Alice, who is thinking about how handsome he is. If they weren't together, she would find him attractive with his silky hair, blue eyes, natural elegance, and loving smile. The way he speaks, takes an interest in others, and talks about his plans and dreams. He moves closer to her and inhales her. *That perfume drives me crazy; it's always the same, wafting after her, all-consuming and intoxicating, like a nectar—perhaps I'm bewitched by her smell. Oh yes, dance my beauty, oh so beautiful, what else is there for us to hope for? Does desire remain when love dies? Does love leave when desire disappears—or does it, in fact, bloom, freed of its rags, of this human shell that gets the better of us?*

4.
Venice, May 2002

"Come on," Alice says as she fixes her husband's tie, "hurry up! We have to leave."

Jules looks at his reflection in the huge rococo mirror in the middle of the lounge, a bright halo in their hotel suite. He's happy with what he sees: a tanned, smooth face, hair brushed back, thin lips, and a broad smile. His eyes sparkle when he sees his wife in a black dress, cinched at the waist, like a the 1950s style when they first met. Her dark eyes, slightly quivering lips, and fists clenching anxiously, she's on edge and full of emotion on the day her son is getting married. Jules looks at Alice intently. He smiles when he notices how overwhelmed she seems, even though he doesn't know the real reason for her inner turmoil.

She is well aware that she'll see him again this evening. That the man whom she loved in secret will definitely be at the party. And her heart—beating like a drum in her chest as though trapped in a prison—is telling her it has stopped beating for him. Why does the thought that he'll be near her make her feel so anxious? Does she still want him? Will Jules finally realize? And how will they react when they see each other again, in public, in front of everyone? Under no circumstance must this relationship be discovered, at all costs. And especially not by their children, who would never forgive them, ever.

"I'm ready," Jules says. "I look ridiculous in these trousers, don't I?"

"You know very well that the in-laws like tradition, especially the mother-in-law!"

"I saw the way you look at them."

"And?"

"It's like you're measuring them up," he says.

"No, it isn't!"

"And your daughter-in-law . . ."

"What about her? I like her a lot."

"Yes, I'm sure you do. Only you just can't bring yourself to speak to her."

"That's not true; we went shopping together," Alice protests.

"Tell the truth, you haven't been able to stand her since the first day you met her. Your expression when Alex brought Nelly home! I'll never forget it."

"I had the impression he wasn't in love with her."

"Who can tell? You were outraged that your son had dared to do that to you. Have another woman in his life!"

"You're wrong, Jules. I really liked the last one—what was her name? Laura?"

"Sarah."

"I never understood why they split up. They were good together."

"She left *him* because of his terrible character."

"And he was on the rebound when he fell into Nelly's arms."

"You see, you don't like her."

"Have you thought about your speech?" Alice asks.

"I haven't prepared anything," Jules says. "I'll improvise."

"You could have written something. I can't believe you haven't. But I told you to come up with something . . ."

"I didn't have time."

"And what do you mean by that? Didn't have time for your son?"

"Why are you so on edge?" he asks.

Jules looks at her, curious all of a sudden. She's worked up, doesn't know what to say, and tries to justify herself.

"It's a special day," she replies.

"Don't worry, Alice. It'll be perfect. You look beautiful this evening. Truly sublime. Have you changed your hair?"

He walks over to her, embraces her, slides his hand down to her hip, and pretends to undress her; she laughs, caresses him, and returns his kiss. He is amazed to see her looking so attractive; he imagines it's for him. So their mouths meet, and their bodies entwine. His hands skim her, examine her, sculpt her. He wants her, lusts after her, seeks her perfume, the sweetness of her skin.

All of a sudden, he embraces her, holds her tight, carries

her to the sofa, and lays her on it, as light as a feather. But a clumsy movement knocks over the lamp sitting on the desk, and the pretty Art Deco shade shatters into a thousand tiny shards on the floor.

"Jules!" Alice cries, startled. "What have you done?"

"Oh, sorry . . . I'm sorry . . ."

Alice rushes to pick up the pieces, but all that remains of the lamp is the pewter base. She tries to pick up the bigger pieces but can't; she tries again using a tissue and cuts herself. Blood drips from her fingers, and she can't stop the flow.

"Wait, I'll help you," Jules says as he takes her hand. "You have to apply pressure."

"It's a disaster," she shouts, crying.

"No, it isn't! I'll get a bandage," Jules says, "It's nothing."

"Not me, the lamp! What you've just done is a disaster!"

"I'm sorry . . . I really am. But why did you even bring it?"

"Are you being like this on purpose? I wanted to give it to Alex and Nelly."

"Really? I didn't know. I couldn't figure out why you'd brought it. I thought that maybe you were afraid there wouldn't be enough light in the hotel room."

"You're such an idiot sometimes. And so clumsy. I can't believe you broke it."

"Alice, please forgive me . . ."

"No, Jules. It's irreparable."

"I'll look everywhere for another one," Jules says, kneeling. "I'll go to every Art Deco antique shop in the world.

I'll find one, whatever it takes. Exactly the same, identical, a sister lamp, or if necessary, the soul mate of this lamp, its alter ego, its twin, a copy. I promise. Alice, please, don't work yourself up into such a state!"

But Alice is in tears, shaking uncontrollably. She eventually takes the glass of water Jules offers her. She was so attached to that lamp. It's the very manifestation of a time that no longer exists, a reminiscence that only survives through these kinds of objects, vestiges of the past. Each time they had moved from place to place, she had wrapped it up carefully to make sure it didn't get broken. And now, with one clumsy gesture, he had destroyed everything.

"Nothing can ever replace it, Jules. What's lost is lost."

Alice swallows her tears, remembering the man she'll see again this evening. She wants to look good for him. She's afraid he'll be disappointed. She wonders if she looks older. If this shattered lamp is a sign or a symbol. She has been trying to resist the passing of time for years. She had tried on ten outfits before choosing a dress and a hat, had been to the hairdresser, and is sporting a bob that frames her face nicely. She has lost weight, does yoga almost every day, and regained the figure she had when she was younger. With her slim legs and her body wrapped in a snug-fitting, stylish body-con dress, she tries to hide her emotions.

The terrace of the hotel where the wedding party is being held overlooks the Venetian Lagoon. Jules and Alice sit with Nelly's parents: Jules funny and affectionate, and Alice reserved. The Adriatic Sea stretches out before them, calm and voluptuous, lapping as the vaporetto sail back and forth between the Lido and St Mark's Square. In the twilight, where the land and sky merge, the houses look like they are dancing on a mirror, reflected in a playful mix of enchanting hues as the last rays of sunlight sink into the water.

Alice is moved by the setting, the balmy breeze, the sea spray, and the alcohol. Unsettled, she hears his sweet nothings, whispered in her ear during that stolen weekend when they had fled like thieves from their own lives. For once, they had felt free to kiss in public, get a hotel room, and enjoy a night of pure pleasure, a unique moment that was their secret, which would only happen once in a lifetime. In Venice, she had discovered a man who was sensitive, tender, intense, respectful, and spontaneous. She had let herself be swept up by a feeling that carried her away, that tore her apart, crushed her.

Jules chats and jokes with the guests. Witty and charismatic, everyone likes him. When he talks about his work or his new passion for archeology and ancient peoples, his audience is captivated. He is both present and elsewhere at the same time, between two worlds, two dreams, two desires, caught between two fires, elusive. He is handsome, untouched by time; he exercises to stay in shape while his brother has allowed his weight to creep up with age, resembling their father Jo more and more.

Jules laughs with Maurice, slaps his back, and puts an arm around his shoulders. With his gray hair and blue eyes, he has the same face as Jules, who whispers something in his ear that makes him laugh. Then he talks about their father, who passed away ten years earlier. He was the one they turned to, the one who they asked for advice. Loyal to his communist beliefs, he had encouraged his sons to get into politics. Maurice is pleased he never did, but Jules would have dearly loved to climb the ranks of the Socialist Party before he distanced himself from it.

Alice isn't herself this evening. Overwhelmed and almost intimidated, she walks over to Auntie Josette who has just arrived, elegant and cheerful, in a wheelchair. She dons a smile, which is unusual for her, on this day when Alexandre is marrying Nelly. She compliments him on his suit, which shows off his slim silhouette, his white shirt contrasting with a Bordeaux tie, his long hair flattened back, and his warm, slightly shy smile when he sees the bride light up the night in her immaculate dress. Nothing escapes Auntie Josette, especially not Alice's distress, which she attributes to a disagreement with Jules. Oh no, it's nothing, Alice says. It's the wedding this evening.

Leaning on the guardrail, Jules and Maurice look out at the sea. Jules thinks about what he's going to say during the speech he hasn't prepared. He knows exactly why: He finds it hard to talk to Alexandre. As soon as they see each other, tensions rise at the slightest word, like they're both ready to explode with rage. The disagreements and reproaches bubble up to the extent that he can't take it anymore, that he has fled to find peace elsewhere, avoid problems, leaving his wife to take care of it. Alexandre has only ever done as he pleased. He stopped studying in tenth grade and failed his high school finals; then when he passed, he went to university to study law and failed the first year. When would he find his way? And there were the fits of hysterics, the tears, the teen crises, the financial crises—there was always drama. What had he done wrong as his progenitor? Hadn't he brought him up well? Had he been absent, not given him enough attention, not been enough of a father, or perhaps too much of one? Alice criticizes him for being too lenient and for having been too libertarian. When Alexandre was small, he had never set any boundaries. Later, when he stopped his studies to devote himself to a career as an artist, he'd let him. When he opened a restaurant, he encouraged him and then helped him financially when he decided to get married. But for how long? Émilie, on the other hand, had always been more independent. She was a violinist and often traveled with her orchestra. She has come to the wedding with her new boyfriend, an Englishman she met at a concert in London. With her hair up in a bun, she's wearing a black fitted dress that shows off her slim figure, like her mother, and a happy smile that lights up her face.

Alice remembers her own wedding, which feels like a long time ago now. Is Alexandre as madly in love with Nelly as Jules was with her when they met? She looks for her husband, and their eyes meet. He always needs to know where she is; he can't bear to be away from her for more than ten minutes without knowing what she's doing or if she needs anything. He can easily spot her in a crowd, the way she walks, the way she moves. Smiling and elegant, she welcomes the guests.

As she greets them, one by one, she can't help but keep an eye out for the arrival of the man for whom she is waiting, yet also dreading seeing again. She pretends to be busy so that the moment isn't dragged out; she moves away to protect herself better, turns on her heels, and looks around for other people she knows, whom she rushes to greet, to put on a front and make sure she doesn't let anyone see how ill at ease she is. Then she catches Jules' eye. She thinks he has figured it out, but no, she knows he doesn't have a clue. He's just watching her the way he always does, like he's following her. He smiles at her, comes over to her, and puts an arm around her waist as Alexandre comes over to greet them with his wife.

"Mom, Dad, you are an amazing couple," he says. "Ever since I've known you, you've never gone a day without arguing. And you're still here, together, as much in love as at the beginning. Nelly, I wish us a life together like our parents have had. Dad, it's over to you! And please keep it brief; I need to go to the toilet, thanks."

Out on the terrace, at the tables decorated with bouquets of white flowers from the countryside, Alice can't take her eyes off her son or hold back her tears looking at the young man he has become.

She misses those times when he was a baby and so attached to her that he couldn't bear it when she left the room. Or later, when she would take a bath or go to the toilet and he would be waiting for her outside the door. The afternoons when she took him to the park. He grew up and became an adorable, affectionate boy, a horrible teenager, and an angry young man. Who is he really? She doesn't know him. Does his wife Nelly know him?

Jules gets up. With a sense of presence and devotion, he smiles at Alice, seeking her approval.

But she's looking at another man, in the complicity of a well-kept secret, an unspeakable taboo, something delightful yet monstrous. If only the others knew. It's like a shiver, a desire to turn everything on its head, to bring out into plain sight something that cannot be said. Again, they look for each other and avert their gaze when Jules speaks into the microphone, entirely at ease and happy to have found an audience.

"To be honest, we've been waiting for this moment for a long time. It's because . . . it was extremely difficult to marry him off. Yes, Nelly, you should know. Quite simply, we had given up hope. We thought he'd never manage it. No one wanted him, Nelly! It's the best day of our lives! Our house is no longer a hotel or restaurant, no more pumpkin tagliatelle or other disgusting recipes, no more holidays by the sea for his benefit, no more conversations with him going, 'What am I going to do with my life?' 'She dumped me,' 'Does she still love me?' 'I'm uncomfortable in my own skin,' 'I'm never going to find a job,' 'I hate you,' 'I want to leave,' 'I can't stand you,' or 'Leave me alone!' And the best thing about it all, Nelly, is that I'm finally going to be able to turn his room into an office! I've only been waiting for twenty years!

"But it's all so overwhelming that I've almost forgotten to mention the most important things and to welcome our dear guests. I won't thank those who have come from afar, very afar even . . . from Spain, Italy, America. It's astonishing to see what people will do to destroy the planet! No, honestly, friends, you should have stayed at home!

"Thank you, Auntie Josette, for having made the effort to join us this evening. It hasn't always been easy between us, but you know that we love you and that we depend on you because, without you, we wouldn't be here. Thank you . . ."

He walks over to her, gives her a kiss, pretends to push her out of her wheelchair, then picks her up and starts his speech again, dusting himself off.

"Alexandre and Nelly, I would also like to say something important to you. When I met Alice, I knew we were going to get married, but I didn't know the amazing adventure we would have. We've done it! There were tough times, highs and lows, unexpected developments, mistakes, and storms, and I'm particularly aware of that this evening, right Alice. You're not going to dump me this evening after this terrible speech, are you?

"Don't forget, Alice, that if you leave me, I'll throw myself into the Adriatic. You know I'm crazy. But sometimes, you have to be crazy to move forward. We had our children. We have gone through this life together, and we'll end it together when our friends are no longer our friends, when our children have left us to lead their own lives, and when they leave us on our own. Perhaps our memories will fail us. We'll definitely lose our hearing and sight, along with our memories. We'll start to become confused, and we'll no longer be able to get up without falling over.

"And on that day, we'll meet again, like the first time, like when we sat on that bench in the Jardin du Luxembourg together almost fifty years ago. And I'll be happy to have spent my life with you as a man who loves and has been loved."

Alice smiles, troubled and moved. The orchestra begins to play *"J'en rêve encore"* by Gérald de Palmas, the guests start to dance, and Alexandre walks to the middle of the room to get Nelly for the slow dance. Alice takes the opportunity to disappear and go for a walk on the beach. She kicks off her shoes. Lights a cigarette. She looks out at the sea, lapping gently, reflecting the light of the full moon. She looks up and contemplates the sky lit up by stars, sighs, overwhelmed, and a little tipsy, having drunk a few glasses to try and dampen her feelings. The joy of seeing her son get married. And the one that no one suspects of seeing that man again, the one who whispered a few words in her ear so sweet she would recognize them anywhere. She turns around and sees the man she had loved, that face with those dark eyes and thick eyebrows, olive skin like it was tanned by the sun. And those lips, smooth and plump, smiling and sad, that whisper ever so quietly,

"So what do you say, Alice? Fancy meeting again here in Venice?"

"When Alexandre told me you were coming, I was worried," Alice murmurs.

"I came for you."

"Why?"

"I never forgot, Alice. That first night, when we slept together, it was like we'd always known each other. Like it was the most natural thing in the world."

"It would never have happened if there hadn't been that trip to Berlin . . ."

"And then . . . Venice. Do you still think about it?"

"Sometimes. I was the one who spoiled it all."

"You felt guilty because you're a woman of duty, and you have built your life on solid foundations."

"And you . . . You wanted to leave your wife, but you stayed. You didn't want to leave. That's what happened, and it's honorable."

"No, it's not honorable. I let everything pass me by . . . above all you. I like you; I like being with you. I love you, and I want to see you again. I don't want to spend my life running after something that I'll never have anymore. I'm too old for that."

Behind them, Alice can see the guests enjoying the party—eating, dancing, Émilie hugging her father, Alexandre—happy tonight—giving him a warm embrace, and Jules looking for her.

"There is something between us. Don't you agree?"

"Wait," whispers Alice, glancing over her shoulder. "Jules is looking for us."

"And? I don't care. I'm going to tell them, everyone. Jules too. I'll talk to him, explain. I'm ready. I was there, Alice, at the Flore. I was there with my cases, ready to be with you."

5.

Paris, September 2001

Alice checks her watch; it's 2 p. m. She has a meeting at 4 p. m., and her heart is racing. Her hands are shaking, she's nervous, and she didn't sleep all night, hesitating, wondering if she has made the right decision—to take control of her life, but what does that even mean, take control of your life? She thinks about her family again, what her children will say—if she leaves them for Paul. She tells herself she shouldn't let their opinion hold her back, yet it does matter. She built her life for them, around them, ever since they were born. They have become her priority, the meaning of her existence. Then she's angry at herself for asking so many questions, pulls herself together, reassures herself, and tells herself she's got nothing to lose. That if they love her, they'll understand. All of a sudden, she thinks Paul won't be there, that he'll have forgotten everything they said to each other seven years earlier. Yet she remembers it all. She feels dizzy; her heart is about to burst. She goes into the lounge and lights a cigarette.

Alexandre comes out of his room. There is a young,

blond, blue-eyed woman with him. She has a short pixie haircut and a round, serious face and looks like she has just woken up, which is no doubt the case: "Mom, this is Nelly. Nelly, I'd like to introduce you to my mother. It's a pleasure to meet you. *Eh*, well, goodbye, thanks, and see you again soon." Introductions made, they leave without further ado, as though they had just greeted the receptionist in a hotel where they had spent the night.

Somewhat astonished and angry, Alice walks into the hall. Then, like a robot, she heads toward the office where Jules is working. Absorbed in his plans, he doesn't look up, unaware of what's happening beneath his own roof. It wasn't all that long ago that they had moved into this apartment in Rue de Chevreuse in Montparnasse, getting into debt to buy it. They had been the tenants, and the owners had decided to sell. Alice hadn't wanted to buy it—her newspaper had just been acquired by a group, a redundancy plan was in the pipeline, and it wasn't the time to get into debt—but Jules had insisted so much she had ended up agreeing. He liked the boulevard with its little shops, cafes, and restaurants, the fact they were twenty minutes from the Jardin du Luxembourg they were in the habit of visiting, where they enjoyed going for a stroll to get some fresh air or sitting on a bench at the pond where children sailed little boats in the wind. They often went to the cinema just below their apartment. They had seen *Amélie*, *The Pianist*, and *Lost Highway* and discovered a passion for Baz Luhrmann, having loved *Ballroom Dancing* and *Romeo and Juliette*. But this afternoon, it is clear that Juliette is getting ready to leave Romeo. In a strange back-and-forth, he has chosen this precise moment to tell her that he wants to talk to her. Obliged to sit down opposite him, she is chomping at the bit, impatient, wanting only one thing: to get it over with since she has decided to leave.

Jules sits down at the large coffee table covered with books and newspapers. Against the wall, there is a bookcase full of books about history, politics, and science, as well as literature and philosophy, that he bought on his meanders through bookstores and past bookstalls, looking for that rare book on universal thought, as though it would fill a gap in his life and give it meaning. He was becoming a mystic, mysterious, and poetic, while Alice, more pragmatic, was starting to worry they would never have the space for it all.

Alice walks to the window and pulls aside the gray blinds and sheer curtains to let in some fresh air. She looks down at the passersby on Boulevard du Montparnasse, at the junction with Boulevard Raspail with the cafes and cinemas. The constant activity, day and night, gives her newfound hope when her heart fails her—and her heart is failing her right now.

She has packed a bag, just one, to avoid raising suspicion. As a precaution, she prefers to be early. She has put on some makeup, foundation, and blush to look radiant even though she's deathly pale, tamed her mid-length dyed brown hair, put on a pretty dress and ankle boots, and packed a few clothes and books in the bag she uses for weekends away.

She has made her decision, and nothing will change her mind. She is in love with Paul and wants a life with him. The only thing she's afraid of is turning up to their rendezvous alone. That she'll be there but he won't, that he won't come, that she'll feel like an idiot, ridiculous, desperate and fragile, dumped. So she'd rather not say a word to Jules and simply leave. If Paul isn't there, then she'll come home like nothing ever happened. If he turns up, as she hopes he will, then she'll tell her husband everything. She can already picture the scene. *I'm leaving Jules. I can't take this anymore. You're never here. And even when you are, you're somewhere else. Where are you anyway? You seem to have new friends, but I've never met them. Who are they? What are you working on so late at night? Who are you? I certainly don't know. Do you even know yourself? Are you even there when I try to talk to you about our money problems and you're staring into space? Where is the man from the white bed of our wedding night, who married my body and my soul? What are you thinking about when you kiss me—less and less often? Do you even know where you are?*

I'm somewhere else, too, on my way to another life. I'm in love with another man. He surprises me, communicates, and communes with me in this strange ritual that we play together in silence. Kissing, embracing one another in silence. Discovering each other, impatient and eager. He's enthralled when he listens to me and is interested in what I have to say, while you don't even hear me anymore or barely look at me, only vaguely interested or frankly irritated. What binds me to him is consuming my heart and making me lose my mind.

Do I have to confess it to you, Jules? I would give our whole life together for a single minute with him. Something physical and spiritual binds us, nurturing me and bringing me back to who I really am. I love the sensation of his hands on me, his eyes seeing me, his lips on mine, this feeling, ever more intense and pressing, that I want all of him. I have found the love of my life, and I can't stay with you anymore because I can no longer bear the loneliness I feel when we're together. I have never felt so good without you. Do you understand what I'm saying? Yet you do know. It's not just a fling or a rebellion—it's a revolution. And if I don't do it now, at my age, I'll never change. Leave me the little strength I still have; I beg you, let me leave.

"So what is it?" she says as she sits down. "You wanted to talk?"

"I'd like to take you to Naples."

"Why?"

"Because it's Naples."

He looks at her with his blue eyes, full of affection and indulgence, trying to seduce her but irritating her slightly.

"I know. I've been absent a lot recently. Haven't I?"

"Yes."

"My work . . ." he begins.

"Yes, your work, of course. Your sites. Your trips, and then politics since you've been involved in that too."

"I've always been interested in politics."

"Well, everything's an excuse to leave the house. Even when you're here, you're absent."

"Listen to me, that's all over."

"Why?"

"I've got the feeling I'm not left-wing anymore," he explains.

"You're . . . right-wing?"

"No. You know very well I've always been left-wing . . . I am left-wing. But not this left-wing that's no longer left-wing. Do you understand what I'm trying to say?"

"You're a communist?"

"Maybe, after all, like my father. Unbridled hyper-capitalism is going to destroy the planet."

"Well, I can agree with you on that, Jules."

"You know, no one really knows what stage we're at. To be honest, I don't even know if the left will make it through to the runoffs next year."

"You're still worried about that," Alice says, looking at her watch. "Since Mitterrand was elected, you see power as a given right."

"I'm not interested in power. And what's all this double-speak anyway?"

"It comes from living with you . . ."

"Thank you for that. But you know what? I don't care. I don't have an ideology anymore. And . . . I think we should make love again, you and I."

"What, Jules? What's that got to do with it?"

"You heard me. I can't get swept up by any sort of ideal as long as there's nothing between us."

"You know," Alice says, "lots of couples stop making love after they've been together for years; that's what I hear from friends. And you know what I hear? It's their fear."

"Fear of what? And what friends are you talking about?"

"The fear of finding themselves in bed at night with their wife, that's what terrifies them the most. They've lost all desire for each other; they end up like brothers and sisters."

"And what do you think of that?" he asks.

"Listen, it's not a problem for me, or at least it isn't anymore."

"We're no longer a couple if we don't make love."

"That's what you think? I don't believe in relationships anymore. I've already tried; we're not going to start afresh, make that mistake," Alice says.

"What are you talking about?"

"Us."

"What are we if we aren't a couple?" Jules asks.

"We're partners."

"That's nothing," he replies.

"It's nothing, and it's everything. They are people who live together, help each other, and co-parent. It's already something."

"For pity's sake, Alice, stop using all those buzzwords. We can't turn back time, but we could make love once a week, or once a month . . . or once a year, couldn't we?"

"But what's got into you all of a sudden?" she asks.

"Firstly, I think you're stunning; you are more and more beautiful."

"No! That's not true. That's enough nonsense. I'm getting older and older. Every day, I see more wrinkles, my skin is sagging, my cheeks are getting hollow, my breasts are drooping, and that makes me anxious. You can't imagine how anxious that makes me."

"So what? That touches me and makes me want you," Jules says.

"Are you twisted?"

"You always have to be ironic. You could say, 'Long live me, long live love!' The one who transcends bodies, old age, time."

"I can see that you've progressed a lot, and that's a good thing. But you see, I've suffered too. I've had to protect myself. And I've changed," she says.

"I think you're having an affair."

"What makes you say that?"

"Alice? Tell me the truth."

"You know, at my age . . . I've given up sex. I spend my time on other things, spiritual and intellectual things, more interesting things. So that works out well; I don't think you're interested anymore. Do you remember what you told me a few years ago?" she asks.

"I don't remember. So what's the point in bringing it back up now? You always look to the past. What I'm interested in is the future, what we're going to build now, together."

"We have gone through so much, and it's already a pretty good achievement to have managed to live together, have children, and watch them grow up. So many years, so many seasons, so many changes . . . Let's not ask too much.

It's a miracle we're still here in this lounge, talking to each other, don't you think?"

"What do you mean?"

"I'm leaving, Jules."

"I know," he says after a pause.

He looks at her, serious, a tragic air about him, on the edge of the precipice.

"I understand, Alice. You've prepared everything; you even opened your own bank account. I read your mail the other day."

"You've been spying on me?"

"I had my suspicions, yes," he admits.

"You've no right to do that. To spy on me."

"I have the right. You know that there is no theft between spouses."

"You don't have the right to open my mail. That's . . . that's an intrusion of privacy. That's something no one can stand. Are you listening to me?"

"Are you going . . . far?"

"You don't need to know."

"When are you coming back?"

Jules looks at her, lips quivering.

"When?"

Alice is anxious. She wonders what he knows, and she doesn't know what to do now or say.

"Tell me everything," Jules says. "It would be easier. Is there someone else? You're not happy with me. You are the mother of my children. I respect and admire you, but

I don't make you happy. Perhaps you've found a man who will love you and whom you'll love?"

Jules looks at Alice tenderly, full of nostalgia.

"But I miss you," he says. "I miss us."

Alice thinks of Paul. It's been seven years since they last spoke. One evening, she felt the need to call him; he had turned off his phone. It seemed normal that he didn't answer; he was married and didn't need to be contactable at any time of the day or night. That was their arrangement. But she couldn't stand it anymore. So, she had only been there to offer him pleasure, breathing space, and happiness so he could cope with life with his wife. She didn't want to go on holiday with her husband anymore, but she still wanted holidays like everyone else. She was annoyed at Paul for not being there when she needed him or when she simply wanted to see him. And worse still, complaining that she was going away with her husband, wasn't that taking the cake? When she had told him that Jules had bought tickets to Naples, he had such a fit of jealousy that she'd had to cancel their trip, pretending something had come up at work.

And those calls on the landline at home, whispering, "How are you? What are you doing? Shall we meet up? When? Tonight? Now, at the cafe across the road? No, not across the road, a bit further away, I'm on my way." Jules caught her by surprise one evening while she was waiting at a cafe not far from their place, and he asked her who she was meeting. And when Paul arrived, she didn't know what to say, her heart pounding. He had noticed she was nervous, but Paul had explained they were organizing a birthday present for him. Jules had believed him, or at least he pretended to.

Those secret rendezvous, confidences. The alibis, quick exchanges, stifled questions, when are we seeing Paul, oh, he's coming for dinner, and what is he doing tonight, next week, next month, next year, in a next life?

The last time they had seen each other, she had told him, "Don't call me again. This time, I've had enough. It's too hard, and I don't want a double life that I can't stand either. We have to end it, even though I love you." And he had replied, "Let's agree to meet in seven years' time at the Flore at 4 p. m., and if we're both there, we'll know that we're destined to be together."

The Café de Flore, with its red canework chairs and green tables out on the pavement, on Boulevard Saint-Germain, where they met for the first time, surrounded by students, St. Germain intellectuals, and lots of tourists. A warm, deep voice, a handshake. The moment when this affair had started. A smile is the unexpected first sign of complicity, something strange and magnetic, and recognition, like the need to talk without having anything to say.

And now, she's taken aback by her husband's speech. Did he feel it? Did he know? She can't quite understand what he wants, as he's sitting there talking to her, looking her in the eye, everything, nothing, as though trying to fill the silence.

She thinks about Paul, his life, and his apartment in the VIIth arrondissement, where she went when his wife and children were away on vacation. The office where he works, the tidy bedrooms belonging to his oldest son and his daughter—she knew that unshakable order shouldn't be disturbed. The lounge with the photos of him and his wife, their heads touching. The wedding photo on the chest of drawers, in which they're young; her smile radiant, his a little contrite. Marie-Claude, impeccable, perfect hair, make-up, clothes organized in her closets, splendidly ignorant of her muddled life where she loves him, and he replies I love you too, darling. He can't stand an untidy house. Everything must remain in its place. His furniture, his papers, his files, his books, his wife, his children. How could he ever leave that perfect life?

After she had broken it off, she put on a brave face for months so she wouldn't cry in front of Jules. She had fled him, said she was busy, and then started drinking. He had been patient; it hadn't been easy for him to put up with her without knowing anything. And the kinder he was, the more guilty she felt toward him.

And now Jules was saying, I love you, I want you, I'm in love with you.

"I love your soul. The way you see the world. I love who you are. Not just your body. But your body, too, of course."

It had been a long time since he had said anything like that to her. She often felt transparent, or that he didn't see a thing, didn't hear what she was trying to say. He was always absorbed in his work. Since he had expanded his business, he had taken on project after project but refused to hire more staff because he wanted to control everything, running his office with only a draughtsman and an engineer. He would visit sites from eight in the morning and then have a string of meetings with private clients about extensions, new buildings, renovations, or with local authorities about plans for multimedia libraries, auditoriums, and even a school in the north of France. By 1 p. m., he would be back at his desk, sketching designs, working on plans, and applying for building permits. At the end of the day, he would meet his teams of electricians, plasterers, and carpenters to make sure everything was going well on the sites with the laborers and general contractors. He no longer had time for her, for them, for the children. Sometimes, he would say they should go out, spend time together, go away for the weekend, but he flees her—and then holds her back when he senses she's running away from him. He doesn't understand that she is somewhere else, that she no longer loves him like she once did, that she doesn't love him anymore—since she changed, started to live a double life, and found herself again since he lost her.

She wants to confess everything and tell him the truth. Every day, she comes back home to their place, unable to smile. Going home stresses her and hurts her. She immerses herself in daily tasks; she has every reason in the world to flee him. She works more and more. Since the advent of the Internet,

she's responsible for both the print and online editions

of the newspaper. She decided to focus more on life in the office as opposed to her work as a roving reporter, so she doesn't travel anymore, covers social and political issues, and is able to take care of the children. But she's afraid of the future, of being fired by the newspaper where she works more and earns less, works day and night, looking for topics, people to interview, and texts to write. Her managing editor asks her to cover "events," which look more and more like human interest stories. Her profession is going through huge changes, but Jules doesn't even realize it. They lead parallel lives. They could go on like this for another twenty years without ever crossing paths. They make themselves believe they are a family, a relationship, a couple. He doesn't know anything, hear anything, or want anything apart from being left in peace when he comes home in the evening. She often wonders how they manage to live like this.

She thinks he doesn't have much respect left for her: He thinks she's depressed, that she's caught up in complicated situations at work, her turbulent relationship with her managing editor, and her money problems.

"How do you see the future?" Jules asks.

"I like Jospin a lot, but I'm not sure he'll be able to win. People have changed. Times have changed. The far right is on the rise; I don't think the party will last. If you want my opinion, we're set for years of the right . . . or worse. The far left is the legacy of the left . . . of your left."

"That's not what I mean. I mean us."

She looks at her watch again; it is 2.20 p. m. She's baffled by this question, as though nothing had happened, as though it was perfectly natural to be sitting there together, as though Jules hadn't caused her all this pain. All of a sudden, he's thinking about the future and saying everything she has wanted to hear for years. All of a sudden, he's talking about them and using that word again: us.

"And what are you expecting from us?"

She remembers those moments on the phone with Paul—when they would quickly hang up, when his wife or her husband would suddenly appear and they invented codes. They were living a secret life, hidden behind lies, like spies, a love that must never be brought out into the light of day. Mundane, outdated, almost pathetic.

We've got the best of it, Paul had said. We don't have the humdrum, the daily worries, the routine, children, and everything that entrenches love. We've got the best part.

Dreams too. Dreams that become memories. A beach, a hotel room on a wild, windy island—who cares if the sea is murky? You never know why these things happen.

Celebrating the moment in all its intensity, strength, and brilliance. That exhilarating feeling when they met, like it was a miracle. Even when they went home, back to their own places, lead-footed, hearts rejoicing.

For a moment, Jules looks at her, and she feels that he has understood. She wants to say it, to tell him. She starts to speak, mumbles a few words, gets up to focus, and starts to tidy away the plates. He joins her, comes to help her, leans over the dishwasher, and gives her the cutlery as he empties it before filling it again, restarting the same infinite cycle.

She realizes that he wants to know. That he's ready. So he asks her how she sees the future. What has gotten into him after two years of not doing a single thing for her, not an iota of attention, a single gift, a word, nothing?

She starts the eco cycle and checks her watch again. September 11, 2001, 2.30 p. m. Seven years ago, exactly. Seven years since she last saw Paul. The children have grown up, and she is older. There are more wrinkles across her face and gray hair, and the years have passed. When they were seeing each other, it had been the opposite—everything went so quickly, the years fell off her, she had been happy and active, and she had dashed from one place to the next.

She gets up, trembles, falters. She doesn't know what to say or do. She hesitates, always hesitates, all the time, about everything. This time, she's leaving. She has decided; she knows she wants to follow her desire. But just as she walks toward the door and opens it, she hears a cry of astonishment.

Or rather horror. Jules is listening to the radio, flabbergasted. A voice is commenting on a news bulletin that is so terrifying it seems unreal. They listen without understanding, without managing to picture what is happening: At 2.46 p. m. today, September 11, 2001, the Twin Towers have been struck by two planes in New York.

Alice retraces her steps, goes into her bedroom, opens her bag, and it's only then that she sees the letter that has been slipped into it. The letter that Jules had written to her the day after they first met, that he had probably put there without her noticing, to let her know that he had understood everything—and to leave her one last message.

6.

Paris, December 1998

Jules carefully takes the letter from the bottom of the drawer where he had hidden it. When they first met, he had found the words to express his bewilderment, his utter bewilderment at having met her at that point in his life.

And he had told her. How on earth had he dared do such a thing? Had it been madness? Had it been love? Would he have written that letter today if they had met in the same way? And the courage, the desire, the burning need to spend his life with her: Would they have been as strong?

Why had it come this far? How had they reached this point? What centrifugal force had drawn them apart after they had done everything, including the impossible, to be together? Was it the children? Their work? The mere fact of living under the same roof and unable to stand each other anymore? An unfathomable sense of nostalgia suddenly overcomes him as he remembers their youth, their good looks, the innocence of their love when they first met on that particular day.

Why does he always return to that moment when they recognized each other and said nothing because it was neither the time nor place? Their affair had caused so much pain and turmoil; they'd had to overcome so many obstacles and survive so many trials—will this be the last one?

He folds the letter up and hides it at the bottom of the desk drawer again. He doesn't want Alice to see it and take it back. This letter is a relic, he thinks, evidence, the vestiges, a monument. All that remains of their first encounter. Bearing testimony to their love for each other.

"Have you thought about how we're going to divide everything up?" Alice asks, appearing in front of him as he slams the drawer shut.

It's already winter, and she's wearing the jeans she likes to pair with a wool sweater and ankle boots. Her hair is up in a "messy bun," as she likes to call it. She looks tired and isn't wearing any lipstick or makeup. Her skin is pale, her face drawn, and her eyes teary.

They decorated the open plan living-dining room with a large sofa, armchairs on either side, a frosted glass table that Jules made himself, and all manner of objects that he chose, one by one, some they had picked up at a Sunday flea market in Saint-Ouen, pictures of Parisian streets, the ones they often used to walk along, hand in hand. The Pont Marie on a foggy autumn morning, and the buildings with high windows looking down over the Seine. The Odeon Theatre, where they had seen plays. The Rue de Rivoli that the wild group of rollerbladers take over on a Friday night, music blaring. What happened to those long walks across Paris' bridges and along the banks of the Seine, crossing from one side to the other, heading toward the Eiffel Tower through the city's gardens? From the left bank to the right bank, the hidden paths through Montmartre, those dark, narrow streets, picturesque and majestic. The Quai des Célestins beneath the arches of the Palais-Royal. The booksellers on the banks, in April or May, with their books and posters on display. Or the Blomet swimming pool in the XVth arrondissement, with its booths around the pool, where they used to swim for an hour. The Sundays, when it was nice weather and they would take a picnic to the Ile Saint-Louis and eat lunch beside the water, next to the bateau mouche, like a Parisian postcard. And, of course, the Jardin du Luxembourg, where they liked to go for a walk, in any weather, in love, for fun, for nostalgia, for the feeling of being in the countryside, for the green chairs, for the dreams and conversations—so many memories.

Émilie is in her room, sprawled out on her bed, listening to her Walkman. She has papered the walls with posters of her favorite pop stars, Madonna and the Spice Girls. In Alexandre's room, the electric train set has been replaced by an electric turntable he got for his twentieth birthday that he uses to play Michael Jackson and David Bowie records. At the end of the hall, there is a large, square room that has been painted white—the master bedroom. They have added a bed covered with a piece of blue fabric from their trip to Naples, a walnut wood desk full of books and trinkets, a stone from the Berlin Wall, and two nightstands piled high with magazines and books.

How long has it been since they last embraced in this marital bed? Since he had touched her, looked at her, kissed her? What had happened to those embraces when they gave themselves to the other, that magnetic, sensual relationship? That feeling that life had meaning, substance, was real. They had once delighted in their names, jumped to answer each phone call, looked at each other, hands entwined, discovered each other, and caressed each other with a gentle strength. And that passion that had swept up their bodies when they were entwined, thirsting after the other. The pleasure in being together, contemplating each other, thinking they were one and the same flesh, of being wanted, transcended, pierced, like it was the first time, suffering when apart, ecstatic when together. The burning desire, lost through routine and the wear and tear of time, perhaps through living together, had been replaced by the minor fixations of life together that irritate and annoy. Jules gets up early and makes noise, which wakes up Alice who needs her sleep, an otherwise insomniac who roams the house at night, eats, reads, and does the chores. She has low blood pressure, struggles to get up, and suffers from dizzy spells. Jules, hyperactive and suffering from high blood pressure, can't bear doing nothing, doesn't like vacations, can't stay in one place, and always has to be doing something, even during the summer. Jules interrupts Alice in public, and vice versa. Sometimes, they complain to each other about this lack of respect in front of their friends and family, which makes everyone feel embarrassed. Jules doesn't like being contradicted and gets angry. He often launches into lengthy lectures, full of judgment, in front of everyone and listens to himself talking, which annoys Alice. She has stopped eating meat and has a strange relationship with food. She has a phobia of swallowing, which prevents her from eating pieces of food that are too small or stringy, and from taking pills. Meanwhile, she drinks wine every day, gets drunk, and starts talking very quickly, going off on tangents and sometimes becoming aggressive. Jules hates seeing her like that.

Jules has mood swings. He can go from laughter to tears in a fraction of an instant, which is unnerving. You never know which foot you're on with him. Alice is uncommunicative. A dreamer, she escapes into her own world. Jules is so demanding when it comes to decoration, about the lights and paintings, that they end up leaving the walls blank and not doing anything at all. Jules is very sociable, constantly making new friends, but does he have any real friends? He's close to his brother Maurice, and Paul, of course, but Alice doesn't get along with Paul's wife, Marie-Claude, at all. When they meet up, she pretends to be interested in her, but deep down, she's bored. Alice doesn't have any brothers or sisters and is solitary, almost antisocial. Jules is extremely meticulous and can spend an hour getting dressed, picking the right colors and fabrics. He finds it hard to decide in shops. He always wears the same suede jacket that Alice thinks is ridiculous for his age, like other clothes he can't bring himself to get rid of because he can never throw anything away. Jules always forgets Alice's birthday, which annoys her, and he doesn't give her gifts anymore, which makes her sad.

On the other hand, he wishes her Happy Mother's Day, which gets on her nerves. Jules doesn't have a good relationship with his father, Jo, who has become crabby with age. They fight often, which upsets Alice, who has lost both her parents.

When he takes a shower, Jules floods the bathroom. Yet he's obsessive about tidying up. Alice leaves her things lying around the apartment; she's clumsy and breaks tableware every week. Jules never does grocery shopping, and the only time he fetched the children, the supervisor at the school refused to give them to him because she'd never seen him before. Jules changed the car, buying his dream car when he signed a big project: a Jaguar Daimler Double 6, though he won't let Alice use it because he says she drives too fast. In reality, he thinks she's a bad driver, given the number of cars she has sent to the wrecking yard. It should be said that Alice is short-sighted but too vain to wear glasses. She hates planning trips, vacations, concerts, and invitations; she needs artistic license, as she calls it. She hates any kind of obligation, so they end up doing nothing. Alice doesn't like television, while Jules is hypnotized by LCI, the news channel that runs on a loop all day, and regularly tunes into Julien Lepers' *Questions pour un Champion* quiz show on France 3. Alice has a group of friends from the women's liberation movement, the MLF, that meet every week, and others from an environmental activist group. In fact, she can't stand it now when lights are left on, when the household trash isn't sorted, when people fly, that women aren't breaking the glass ceiling, that their salaries are lower than men's, and that they're snowed under every day with work, children, and everything else. Jules often tells the same stories, especially to his friends, stories she knows by heart, memories from his childhood and time in the army. He's been cracking the same jokes for thirty years, word for word. Alice doesn't like cooking, but she's interested in daringly bland culinary experiences like chicken mole or beetroot soup. Every morning, Jules reads the paper, religiously. Alice is a spendthrift and buys on impulse. Jules keeps a very strict budget for household expenses, but he's a collector: He picks up everything from figurines and pens to soap, postcards, and stamps. He's interested in archaeology and brings back strange objects from flea markets and the countries he visits. He piles up books, new ones and old ones. And other things, too, that he locks in a secret cupboard. No one knows what it contains. He puts the documents and files that he works on late into the night in there too. Every Thursday evening, he plays bridge with Paul and a few new acquaintances while Alice goes for dinner with Auntie Josette, who lives on her own. Jules tends to complain about everything, like his father and brother.

Jules and Alice don't make love very often anymore, and when they do, it lacks eroticism—it is a simple mechanical act. It never lasts long and is routine. They barely talk to each other, don't look at each other anymore, don't spend time together, and don't have any meandering conversations anymore, apart from the one enduring topic: "cash," as he says. In those moments, she's amazed she's dealing with someone so miserly, so tight-fisted, and keen to strip her of hers if he can't possess her. She feels like she is discovering him as he is, naked and ridiculous with his tiny nest egg that he clings on to like his entire life depends on it, and deep down, a new feeling is growing in her, one she had never felt before, the most fatal of all passion-killers: scorn. As for Jules, he thinks it's ridiculous for her to get emotional about everything, including the film *Titanic*, which she couldn't stop crying through. She's afraid of the future, of the impending crisis, terrified at the prospect of being fired and losing her job. Since she was hired by an economically liberal newspaper—something that makes Jules' hair stand on end—she has become aware of the crisis affecting the planet. She's afraid of rising unemployment, mad cow disease, AIDS, Dolly the first cloned sheep, and all those computers that have invaded homes and are used as typewriters, but for how long? She can clearly see that they are on the verge of a radical change, a world that is transforming rapidly, along with her own life. Everything she has built could collapse before her eyes, like a house of cards. Her insomnia is getting worse; she's becoming aggressive, irritated, and bitter.

In a cupboard, Alice has stored all the tableware that Jo gave them for their wedding, candlesticks, vases, figurines, vacation souvenirs, all the objects that are part of their life together, collected over time. Embroidered tablecloths bought at flea markets, coffee pots, teapots, old cameras, pictures collected here and there from different stages of their lives, 33 RPM vinyl by Joe Dassin, Nicole Croisille, Frères Jacques, Léo Ferré, Jean Ferrat, piles of DVDs and VHS of films ranging from *The Young Girls of Rochefort* to *An Affair to Remember*, along with documentaries on World War II that fascinate Jules.

She wonders what will happen to this "shared property." Like the lacquered wood piano that Alexandre plays in his spare time while she listens from the sofa in the lounge. And their memories? Can they share those? And the children? Is it possible to cut them in two, or if that's not possible, to separate them—she would take the girl and Jules the boy, or vice versa? When she had told him she was pregnant with Alexandre, he had said he was over the moon. She had smiled at the expression; she was over the moon too, and she suddenly felt much better and important for producing—through the children—plans. But she had been mad at him for his reaction when she had told him she was pregnant with Émilie; surprised, he hadn't expressed the same enthusiasm. He had said it was too soon, that he wasn't ready, that he was working all the time and wouldn't be able to take care of her. There would be a seven-year gap between Émilie and Alexandre, and it wasn't too soon, she had replied; it was too big a gap. It had been a deep wound at the bottom of her heart that had never healed but rather become infected, like all the miscarriages she'd had that hadn't really affected Jules. He hadn't realized that this child was a miracle, the fruit of his desire.

His glasses perched on his nose, Jules drums his fingers on a pile of files, concentrating. Alice stands in front of him.

"So," she asks. "What have you decided?"

"We'll do what we agreed."

"We need to clarify the situation before going to the lawyer."

"We need to be realistic; I don't want to end up penniless tomorrow because you decided you wanted a divorce. So, to find some common ground, we'll have to resolve the issue of the apartment."

"You want to keep it in joint ownership?" Alice asks.

"Of course. But you do realize that means you'll have to repay the share of the apartment covered by the loan from my father to keep your half."

"That doesn't matter," she says.

"Stop saying it doesn't matter because we can't have a discussion like that."

"Okay, we'll do that then," he agrees.

"You're okay with that?"

"We already discussed it, didn't we?"

"We'll discuss it again now since you haven't understood what will happen. I will give you half of this apartment, but we have to decide when and how you'll repay Jo to retain joint ownership," explains Jules.

"We'll repay your father, and that will be it; we'll get rent if we continue to rent it out."

"How will my father get his money back?" Jules asks.

"We'll take out a loan."

"And how will it be repaid?" he asks.

"With the rent," she says.

"And in three months' time, when you're fed up living on your own, you'll say what a pity it is to have an apartment that we can't use."

"Outrageous, actually," Alice replies, tears in her eyes as she looks at him.

"You've just gained an apartment. Aren't you happy?"

"Yes, very happy. And the rest?" she asks.

"The rest is your income for the past three years, anything you haven't credited, and whatever is left in the bank. What do we do with the money you received?"

"I don't have anything left. I spent it all."

"But I can't end up taking out a loan on my own to live off and repay my father while you spend all the money you get!" Jules says.

"Okay, but you know very well how much I earn and that it's not going to increase. Meanwhile, you make my hair stand on end with your complicated calculations," she says.

"What do you mean by that?"

"How much do you earn as an architect? It sounds like you have a slush fund."

"I shall not respond to this underhand criticism, worthy of the far right, which isn't surprising given the rag you work for. And what about you? How much do you spend every day at the pharmacy, in shops, on train and plane tickets that you buy twice because you got the date wrong?" he snaps.

"If we split our assets, it'll be each for their own. So we'll do whatever we want, Jules."

"So we take out a loan to repay my father. But you'll start to tell me that you're giving my father money when it's the opposite. Do you understand my proposal?"

"Of course," she replies.

"So we will need to agree on how to share our assets because I don't want to be the only one trying to cut back while you spend everything."

"So how do you suggest we split everything?" she asks.

"I don't know yet. At the moment, you don't seem to be ready to give up your money, your apartment, or the rest. When you realize how much we need to repay, you'll say it's out of the question!"

"How much is it?" Alice asks.

"A third of what the apartment's worth today. So that's 150,000 euros immediately."

Jules gets up, looks at her coldly, takes his jacket, and leaves the apartment, slamming the door behind him. Alice is left at the desk alone, in pieces. With tears in her eyes, she hangs her head in her hands in utter desperation. Is he trying to do everything he can to prevent her from leaving, or is he quite simply a downright horrible person? She finds him utterly repugnant, physically and morally. She only wants one thing, to leave, but does she really have the resources, and how can she survive on her own?

Alice is sobbing when Émilie comes out of her room, slamming her door, furious. Alice doesn't have the strength to react and would rather lie low, but the young woman comes into the lounge and looks at her mother, frowning ferociously.

She looks like the poster hanging over her bed of Nina Hagen, the German singer sticking out her tongue like a raging shrew. She developed such bad acne as a teenager that her cheeks, now swollen and puffed up with candies, chocolates, and cakes, still bear the scars. She announces that she has decided to go abroad for a year; she wants to drop everything—the violin and the conservatoire. She wants to escape, to take her mind off it all because she's suffocating here.

"Were you fighting again? But why are you still together?" Émilie asks.

Her dyed pink and blond hair frames her face, and her round cheeks are contorted with anger. The young woman, dressed in hole-ripped jeans that expose her thighs and barely contain her stomach, is fuming.

"It's all your fault. You boss everyone around. Wear this, not that. Do it like this, not like that. I'm not a baby anymore. Even when I was small, you would put me in that horrible red bonnet, those mittens, and booties saying that it was to protect me from the cold . . . but what were you thinking? Other than how to make me look stupid in front of my friends? All you do is criticize me and tell me I eat too much, sleep too much, go out too much, and don't work enough. I think you don't love me—that, in fact, you've never loved me because I'm not good enough for you. You think I'm a loser. Not thin enough, not classy enough, not classical enough. All you do is shout at me. And all it does is annoy me. Can't you just think for one moment that we're having a nice time? You always have to spoil everything because you don't know how to be happy, nice, or kind. You're never pleased because you're not happy yourself. And Dad isn't the only one who is fed up with you."

"May I suggest you solve a puzzle?" Alice says. "What is the difference between your bedroom and a huge trash can?"

Émilie slams the lounge door, goes back into her trash can, and gets a chair to block the door. Then she gets her violin and throws it as hard as she can against the door. It explodes. Alice can feel the vibrations right to her core.

Meanwhile, Alexandre has come out of his room and is watching her, a look of fear in his eyes.

"What's going on?" he asks.

Alice looks at him. Twenty-four years old, it's hard to see his face hidden under a head of brown hair, a curly mop he doesn't want to cut, the same way he never really seems to want to work or continue his studies like his parents did.

"Are you leaving? You're dropping us?"

"Who, you?"

"*Eh* . . . Dad and us."

"I'm entirely devoted to you. I do everything for you all the time. Can you understand that, or do I have to remain a prisoner in this house for the rest of my life? I didn't sign up for that. To lock myself up in a cage. I need to breathe, to be free. I've given everything for you two, Alex. I gave up everything. All my ideals, and even my ideas!"

"Which ideas?"

"My feminist ideas. I'm at your service, all three of you. That's all I do. And my life as a woman . . . it's gone. I'm at the end of my tether."

"Where do you want to go?"

"I don't know," Alice says, "but one thing that's sure is that I don't want to stay. Your father is horrible."

"Well, I'm not going to disagree, he has his faults, but . . ."

"If you knew what I've had to put up with. I hide it all, I don't tell you anything, I protect his image, but . . ."

"I forbid you from talking about Dad like that," Émilie suddenly screams, back for more. "You're the horrible one, and you only ever think about yourself."

"No. It's both of us. We're both horrible. Your father and I, we can't stand the sight of each other anymore. We've got nothing left in common. We're living separate lives. Get it? I can't put up with this charade any longer. Can you imagine what it's like? Not being able to stand the sound of someone biting a grape? We're living like animals, in a pack, because we had children together. It's dehumanizing. We don't feel anything for each other anymore, nothing. It's over."

As she says these words, Alice can no longer hold back her tears. They roll down her cheeks without stopping. She remembers the early days when they were in love. What had happened to those eyes that shone and that carefreeness, those feelings expressed in the letter with which he had seduced her? That letter she had reread so many times that she now wants to tear up, to burn. She gets up and looks in the desk drawer. She's sure she put it there, with other important papers, because she had noticed that Jules was looking through her things and taking documents, photos, and even family jewelry he had given her. But she can't find it, so she tries to take off her wedding ring, struggles, and keeps trying. Her hand has thickened, like the rest of her; she hadn't taken it off since their wedding day. And now she can't unless she cuts off her finger.

The phone rings, and Alice jumps up to answer it in front of the terrified-looking Émilie and Alexandre.

"Jules," she says when she picks up. What do you want? Where are you?"

"Outside, in the phone booth. You can see me from the window. Look, it's me waving the telephone directory!"

She goes over to the window and sees him waving at her. She can't help but smile through her tears, seeing him like that down there in the phone box, sheepish, looking at her, pleading.

"I don't know what you're doing with your life, but I don't care," Jules says on the phone. "I love you. I want you to stay. I'm sorry for what I said earlier. I didn't know what to say to make you stay. I don't want you to leave, Alice."

"It's too late."

"What? It's never too late."

"I can't," she says.

"But what are you looking for? What do you want?"

"Why are you hurting me so much?"

"You're crazy," he replies.

"You see, you're insulting me again. There you go again. It's all starting over again."

"Do you even realize! It's only because I'm strong that I hang on. Because you act strangely. Not even that . . . You act like someone who's not well . . . like Josette!"

"Poor soul," Alice rages. "I knew you were a bastard. You know what? Go fuck yourself! You can all go fuck yourselves!"

"I'm sorry," Jules says, crying down the phone. "I'm talking nonsense. I wanted to hurt you, sorry. Stay. Or leave. You can leave if you want or go to another room—or another apartment if you prefer. Let's just find some sort of arrangement, I beg you. I'm nothing without you, Alice. I love you with all my heart, with all my soul. Without you, my life is meaningless. I'll do whatever it takes, whatever you want. If you were to ask me to throw myself under a car right now, I wouldn't hesitate. That's a terrible thing to stay; that wouldn't make anyone want to stay. I don't know what to say. It's not too late, Alice, I beg you, let me prove it to you."

7.
Paris, September 1994

"I think you are both affected by guilt; that's why your relationship is dysfunctional," Dr. Bansard says.

Jules holds back a skeptical smile, Alice looks out the window, and the therapist takes off his glasses and looks at them with kindhearted matter-of-factness. In his sixties, long hair framing his slim face, he observes them through his round glasses from behind his rosewood desk, empty apart from a gray telephone with a round dial and a book he wrote himself, displayed prominently: *Can Love Heal Today?*

"Do you have something you want to tell me?" Alice asks.

But Jules doesn't reply. Looking at her, he is, in fact, paralyzed with guilt. Since he doesn't want to lie, he remains silent to avoid any drama. He is afraid of her: of annoying her, triggering her anger, causing an argument that ends with shouting and door slamming. Ever more on edge and touchy, she's on the defensive, and he can no longer talk to her calmly and in peace, which is why he persuaded her to start couples therapy.

"Well, go on, say it," Alice insists. "It's not that hard."

Jules hesitates and looks at Dr. Bansard, who smiles to encourage him and tell him that it's not actually that bad, that he's in a place where he can express himself freely. So Jules confesses that he feels guilty: for everything and nothing. For betrayal: He's afraid of being punished, despised and rotting in hell. He's heartbroken—for her, his wife and the mother of his children, whom he loves above all. He looks devastated, and Alice starts to get seriously worried.

"Since the change," she explains, "he hasn't been feeling very well."

"What change? You don't live together anymore?"

"The change in government. He's dreamed of getting into politics for a long time, but he can't find his place."

"It's not that, Alice," Jules says, irritated.

"What is it then? I'm ready to hear it. Get it off your chest."

"Yes, it can help to say something," Dr. Bansard says. "To get it off your chest, as Alice quite rightly says. To allow yourself to express what you're feeling deep down. I think Alice is ready to hear it."

"Hear what?" Alice screams. "What on earth are we talking about? I'm ready to hear what?"

Jules doesn't reply. He looks at her, virtually quaking. His left eye is twitching, a nervous spasm, while his right eye tries to woo her.

"Let's see, let's hear what Jules has to say."

Alice gets up, walks to the window, and comes back.

"That . . . you're having an affair?" she asks.

Jules hangs his head.

"You're having an affair, and what do you want? For me to give you my blessing? So you can continue, head high, proud of yourself? Well done! Is that what you want?"

"No. I'd like to talk to you. In a way we've never talked to each other."

"I don't know why, but I don't feel comfortable about this, about this opener."

Silence. Dr. Bansard readjusts his glasses and looks at them in turn, first one, then the other. But they don't say a word. Jules hangs his head in his hands, and Alice looks at him.

"He has something important he'd like to say," stresses the therapist. "Do you understand? He would like to talk to you."

She turns to Jules.

"You've got something you want to tell me? Something to confess? Well, then, go on. How long has it been going on? Where did you meet? Where do you see her? What do you do?"

Sitting on the chairs, in this welcoming room with red curtains and wallpaper and colorful rugs, a fantastical room full of confessions and admissions, in front of the encouraging psychoanalyst, the angry eye of his wife, the gaze of all who inhabit his subconscious, grandparents, parents, friends, and children, before history, the entire Earth listening in that moment, Jules makes his confession. By dint of being together, they have become each other's shadow.

They mumble to each other, half-understand each other, comfort each other, apologize, and no longer have the strength to argue or disagree. They no longer even feel anger. They spend all their time together. They are restricted to their house, their bedroom, and their bed.

His eyes tear up, hands shake, feet tap nervously, and then he finally begins to speak. He tells her everything. The affairs. The lies. The drunken, psychedelic, erotic evenings. They meet in a hotel, take a room for a night, and leave in the early hours. Each time, it's strange being with a body that isn't his wife's. Experiencing that exhilarating moment, which has become a drug, like when you gamble at a casino to get an adrenaline rush, a way of living to the max, on a tightrope, of questioning everything, going all in, like when you play cards. He feels alive when his heart is pounding on his way to meet one of his mistresses in secret. The taboo heightens his desire; the pleasure is intense when it's illicit. He's got his places, ones where he feels good in his turmoil. Sleeping together is an indulgence, not a duty. Nothing is planned. Everything is spontaneous. Sometimes, he goes to their places. The children are there, and they have to be quiet. One night, a baby woke up. Another night, a husband could have come home. That's what you call living dangerously. Yet these are the moments that make him happy again, like he's finally found his place, like he's being reborn.

Where? On his trips out of town, when he visits sites, at the office, anywhere. When? During the day, between meetings, and at night sometimes. Why? It's like time stands still, like he's somewhere else, away from it all. It's the risk of being found out that brings him a strange sense of pleasure. How? Because those one or two hours are so intense, he manages to abandon himself completely; he doesn't have time, so he cuts to the chase. For what purpose? To be one—for an instant. Pleasure, after a lack of it, the absence of it; desire, uncertain reunions. It's about being there, fully, not entirely. While waiting for these encounters, he feels important, and between them, he waits, or pretends to live, holding his breath. These brief encounters have become essential, and this frenzy is a need. He thinks that living like this has prevented him from falling into depression.

There is silence.

"Who?" she asks.

Alice looks at him. Her heart is racing, her legs are weak, and she feels like she's going to faint.

"Who?" she screams. "Give me names! I need names! Faces!"

"What good would names do? I don't even know them myself. I've forgotten everything," he says.

But Alice has a few clues. Searching through her memory and Jules' things, she had found a dedication in a book on his nightstand, *The Joke* by Milan Kundera: *In memory of a crazy night, S.*

Was it Sandrine, her beautician who comes once a month for her treatments, who Jules always greets very warmly? Was it Stéphanie, the secretary at his architect's office, whose southern accent he always parodies? Sabrina, the bookseller he loves and who always recommends books he brings home, armfuls of them for his bookcases? Sonja, his client from the East? Sabrina, his first cousin's wife, who they see once a year at Christmas at his father's, with whom he loves to discuss politics because they don't vote the same way? Sofia, his former associate who went back to Spain and who regularly returns to Paris and always calls in to say hello? Sylvie, the real estate agent who showed them their apartment and took Jules' number but not hers? All of a sudden, the world is full of names beginning with S.

"Where did *The Joke* come from?" she asks.

"It's not a joke," Jules replies cheerlessly.

"That Kundera book you were reading the other day."

"I don't know. I found it in the bookcase when we were moving."

"Did someone give you it?"

"Maybe . . ."

"Jules? Answer me, or I'm leaving you immediately."

"I don't know, I'm telling you."

"There's a dedication inside, Jules. 'In memory of a crazy night, S.' Who is 'S'? And what was that crazy night?"

Jules looks at her, speechless.

"Tell me now, or I'll wreck this office!" Alice suddenly screams, the therapist looking on worried. "Who is 'S'? Your mistress? Who is it, Jules?"

"Calm down," Dr. Bansard says. "Jules is just trying to tell you that he still has desire. And that's the most important thing: staying true to one's desires. Because that's what keeps us alive."

"Would you like me to congratulate him, Dr. Bansard?" Alice asks. "Give him a round of applause?"

"No," Jules says. "I don't deserve to be congratulated. I deserve to have you leave me."

"You want me to leave you because you can't bring yourself to leave?"

"No, that's not what I mean."

"When was the last time?"

"Do you think I should tell her everything?" he asks Dr. Bansard.

"While you're at it."

"This is a strange conversation."

"Well, then?"

"Last year."

"Who was it?" Alice asks.

"That doesn't matter."

"Why are you telling me now?"

"I can't keep it to myself anymore. It's suffocating me, stopping me from living, wearing me down, ruining my life. I can't look you in the face anymore or at my own face in the mirror. Do you understand?"

"You haven't seen anyone since?"

"No."

Alice feels the effect.

"So why did you do it? Why did you do that?"

"To stay alive. I needed freedom. I shouldn't have had this tidy, well-organized, well-ordered life. I built my life around the family. And I set aside my values, everything that made me feel alive, Alice. Do you remember when you told me you were pregnant with Émilie?"

"Yes."

"That's when I lost my grip. One child . . . that's a couple with a child. Two children, that's a family. I hadn't signed up for that. I was a rebel. I was a Trotskyist, a libertarian. I think I was made for something else."

"But for what, Jules? To live in a commune in the Ardèche? On your own like a tramp? Go to Castel every night? Do what with your life? Weren't you satisfied with your houses, hotels, and everyone who bows down to you because you're such a good architect? Such a good architect who hasn't managed to make a name for himself. Who no one mentions, who no one copies. A mediocre architect, in fact. You needed more than that to reassure you, right? Otherwise, why did you do it?"

"Maybe to find out that I've got an amazing wife, even if I'm not amazing myself."

"Do you hear what he's saying?" Dr. Bansard asks.

"What is he saying exactly?"

"Do you love me, Alice? Maybe you don't love me anymore. Right? This summer, we're sending Émilie to a scout camp, and we'll have a month together. We could go to Naples. How about it?"

"But you're ill, Jules," Alice roars, beside herself. "You need to seek treatment. You've just told me that you're cheating on me with I don't know who, I don't even know why. And you want us to go away together. But I never want to see you again, Jules. I want to feel alive, too. I've had enough of you, too, of everything. Of us. Maybe I want a divorce. And maybe I'll find the strength to do it this time. Or rather, to get even. And I mean real revenge. Revenge that will hurt you. And the worst thing is, you'll never even know what it is."

"If I were you, I'd rather divorce."

"No, that would be too kind."

"Is that what you want? War?"

"And what about you? What exactly do you want? You don't want to get a divorce because the situation suits you. You've got a wife, a family, mistresses. It's perfect for you!"

"Well then, let's get a divorce. I'll be the first one to support you."

"I think you're mistaken."

"What?"

"That you're fooling yourself by fooling around on me."

"What on earth do you mean?"

"You think that you're fooling me, but you're fooling yourself by thinking that you're fooling me. And, in fact, the one you're fooling is yourself."

"I don't follow you, Alice . . ."

"Me neither," Dr. Bansard admits, looking puzzled.

Jules looks down, embarrassed. Alice gets up.

"To put it bluntly, you're a scumbag, Jules," she shouts. "You're a filthy scumbag. I detest you. I hate you. I curse your miserable life. I despise everything you are. I never ever want to see you again. Never ever! Do you hear me?"

"Please don't judge me."

"Don't judge me. That's got to be the best thing I've ever heard."

"Stop being ironic. All around me," he says, "everywhere I look, everyone is leaving their wife and children, getting divorced for much less. It's like an epidemic since women started earning a living."

"You're real macho. Leave, that would be better."

"No, I'm staying. Out of responsibility, duty, love, too. I decided to say nothing, for you, for the children. And the air that I breathe allows me to remain free; otherwise, I was suffocating . . ."

"Do you hear what he is telling you?" Dr. Bansard asks.

"Wait a minute, Dr. Bansard, are you an ENT or a therapist?"

Alice gets up, and Jules trudges along behind her. They leave the therapist's together and disappear into Alice's Smart car. She roars off, speeding down the road and scowling without saying a word, at risk of causing an accident. Jules fastens his seatbelt beside her. When they arrive, Alice slams on the brakes and parks between two cars, takes the key out of the ignition, and slams the door angrily, in desperation. They go back home in silence. Émilie is there. She needs help with her homework, but no one can help her.

"What happened? Have you been fighting again? This screaming is unbearable. You have to separate in the long run! I can't take it anymore." In tears, she runs to her room, and they hear her play her violin, music from Schindler's List—loud, beautiful, harrowing.

Alice, struck, opens a bottle of wine, pours herself a glass, then another, smokes a cigarette, then another. Jules sits down beside her and tries to hold her hands, but she shrinks back.

"Stop it," Alice mumbles. "Don't touch me."

"You're tough," Jules says, suddenly afraid. "Actually, you're the one who doesn't love me anymore. Right?"

"And you love me?" she asks.

"I love you more than anything else in the world. You and the children are all I've got."

"How can you say that?" she shouts. "How can you say that and do what you do?"

"I wanted to screw it all up," he says. "I needed it to stay. I'm such an idiot. Hopeless. Please forgive me. I beg you . . . you're my life. I'd give anything for you. Take me back, Alice."

He gets down on his knees, serious, earnest, at her feet; she pushes him away to extricate herself from his embrace. He cries, she trembles, she's overwhelmed, they hate each other, and they no longer know who they are or what they'll become—lovesick, full of doubt, resentment, and anger.

Alice searches the bookcase for a book, finds Dr. Bansard's, and throws it on the floor, then she spots what she's looking for, *The Joke*, and opens it at the dedication written on the first page. Jules doesn't react. Holding the book, she places it in front of him. He takes it, and, surprised, she snatches it back, feels her heartbeat quicken and her heart pound furiously while the blood throbs in her temples. She turns pale again when she rereads the words she knows by heart: *In memory of a crazy night, S.*

She gets up, furious, and suddenly flings the book at the door. She lifts a vase, smashes it, and continues her rampage of destruction through the room. She's sweating; she could hit him, pummel him. She's so hurt that he should take her for an idiot, that he had betrayed her, his wife, the mother of his children.

What should she think? Her friend Sophie always says that when a man cheats on a woman, it's because it's already over, but she doesn't have the feeling that it's over, that they don't love each other anymore. So why? She jumps. Sophie . . . another "S" . . .

"Sophie?"

"What?" he shouts. "You've lost your mind!"

"Well, tell me everything then."

"There's nothing to tell," Jules says.

Alice gets up, takes out the vodka, pours herself a glass, then another one, and downs it.

All night, she tries to extract a confession from him. He doesn't say anything, nothing new, nothing better, nothing apart from that he loves her, that he's sorry, that he's devasted, while she gets drunker and drunker until the alcohol hits. She feels awful and runs to the bathroom, Jules too; he holds her while she vomits, miserable. Miserable with despair, fear, and disgust at having drunk too much. They sit in front of the toilet bowl, looking at each other. He strokes her hair gently and simply tells her he loves her. Tears are shed, but it doesn't matter because he adores her; she is his life, his soul mate, his other half. He can't breathe without her. She is his happiness, a happiness he deserves. So why? He felt rejected; it had been several years since their bodies had searched for each other. She doesn't touch him anymore or look at him. She's not attracted to him. She's actually the one withdrawing from him, and he had to satisfy his desire with other women to survive. But that doesn't justify anything, explain anything, or excuse anything.

"It's true," she says.

"What?"

"I withdrew from you."

Alice looks at him, and all of a sudden, with the alcohol, late hour, and fatigue, she feels like talking to him, telling him everything, too—or almost everything.

"Do you remember that report about the fall of the Berlin Wall?" she asks.

"Yes. I stayed here with the children. It was the first time I was alone with them. When you left, we all looked at each other, and Émilie started to cry . . . I couldn't get her to calm down for three days. Why?"

8.

Paris, November 1989

"Good morning, little girl; I'm the fairy. The Blue Fairy. Do you recognize me?"

Émilie is sitting on her bed, dressed as Belle. Not Belle from *Sleeping Beauty*, who is pink, or Belle from *Lady and the Tramp*, who is a dog, just like the one in the *Belle and Sebastien* cartoon, but in a blue dress like Belle from *Beauty and the Beast*. The little girl stares at the character who has just appeared, like magic, in her bedroom, wearing a long, sparkling blue, silk cape, a mask the same color, and a princess costume. She is so beautiful and so mysterious!

Awestruck, Émilie nods yes.

"You're the Blue Fairy."

"And you're Émilie Jolie. I have come to grant your wishes. What do you wish for most in the whole world?"

The child blinks, too overwhelmed to reply.

"Tell me, my delightful princess, what is your wish? Tell me, and it shall be granted!"

"I don't know . . ."

"Would you like a violin?"

"No," she says, shaking her head.

"Would you like to go to the Asterix Park?"

Yes, the little girl nods.

"Would you like a Barbie doll?"

"I already have one! She's called Clara."

"Clara? What a beautiful name! I'm sure you would like a little sister, wouldn't you?"

Without hesitating, "No!" she replies.

"What would you like then?"

"I want candy!"

"Candy?"

"And a plane!"

"Very well then, Princess Émilie, since you have been so nice, you shall have your wish granted. I'm going to say goodbye now because I have other little girls to visit. You know how I go from house to house to grant wishes for lovely children."

With a nod of her head, the Blue Fairy curtsies and then tiptoes back out of the room as Émilie watches. Once she's back in her room, she undresses, carefully folds up her costume and hides it in a box on top of her wardrobe, pulls on sweatpants, gets out a toy airplane wrapped in gift paper, some candy, and chocolate, and goes back into her daughter's bedroom.

"Good evening, Émilie. Look at what I found at the door! Is it for you?"

Amazed, Émilie pounces on the gifts.

"It was the Blue Fairy!" she says, full of excitement. "It was the Blue Fairy!"

"What are you talking about? Did you have a dream?"

"No, no, it wasn't a dream," says the little girl. "It was a fairy!"

"But you're talking nonsense—fairies don't exist! You'll have to stop watching cartoons. They give you funny ideas."

"But they're real!"

"You must have dreamed it!"

"But you can't understand. You didn't see her; you didn't see the Blue Fairy."

The Blue Fairy joins Jules in bed. He's wearing blue pajamas, perfectly matching both her and the wallpaper—an entirely blue world, like in the Smurfs. It's time to go to bed because the Sandman will be here soon, and Nicolas and Pimprenelle will close their eyes and say goodnight to Casimir, François, Julie, Club Dorothée, Jackie, Miss Piggy, Kermit the Frog, and the rest of the gang in Sesame Street.

Their apartment looks out over Rue Mouffetard in the Vth arrondissement, not far from the Jardin du Luxembourg. Jules renovated it entirely, with three bedrooms and a lounge with a sofa bed, an extremely modern kitchenette, exposed beams that he loves and which regularly knock Alice out when she gets up at night to take care of the crying children who are scared, sick, can't get to sleep, won't sleep, are hungry, thirsty, need a hug, want someone to tell them a story, fighting, or want to play with Playmobil in the middle of the night.

Jules has opened his own architect's office, and they finally have the money to buy furniture, a Renault station wagon, and new clothes for themselves. Alice has discovered soft silk blouses, and Jules a love for cashmere and lambswool sweaters, along with Italian shoes. They occasionally go to small local restaurants where they have their favorite menus and their habits—sole and green beans for Alice, soups and potato gratins for Jules, and breaded fish and fries for the children. For vacations, they pack the car with suitcases, clothes, toys, rubber rings, little boats, ducks, and inflatable paddling pools, check the Bison Futé to avoid traffic jams, get lost in the middle of the countryside along the way, and eventually arrive at hotels or holiday apartments by the sea in France, Spain, or Italy, where they build sandcastles with the children and eat ice creams on the village square in the evening. The sky, the birds, and the sea help them escape from the work they do during the year. The children smile with their hair wet, cheeks salty from the sea spray, and skin tanned by the sun. Alice spends her days taking care of Émilie, playing with Alexandre, dozing under a parasol, and making the most of her husband's presence, who is often absent during the year. He comes home from the office later and later or travels to visit sites while she takes care of the house and children alone.

Alice slips into bed beside Jules; she's happy tonight, exhilarated with a sense of joy she would like to share, paradoxically, with him, like he was her companion, best friend, and brother. In fact, she no longer looks at her husband in the same way. Physical intimacy is either non-existent or too fleeting to be satisfying, and since the children were born, it has become almost incongruous. Everything— absolutely everything—has become desexualized in their world full of dolls, cars, teddy bears, books about Babar and Dumbo, Walt Disney fairytales, and VHS cassettes that have replaced the Hollywood romantic comedies that Alice enjoys. Like *Lady and the Tramp*, they eat spaghetti with tomato sauce and look at each other affectionately, but there's barely any room for winks, kisses, embraces, or inappropriate suggestions in this universe stamped with the magical realism of fairytale characters. They treat each other with respect, humor, kindness, patience, joy, and friendship, hoping that one day . . . but that day never comes. Alice turns away from Jules, who is no longer interested in her body but rather in a thousand and one other things like work, plans, sites, playing bridge, or reading *L'Express*, *Le Monde*, and *Paris Match*. By dint of living with children, they have become big children themselves. They call each other Mom and Dad. They go to bed exhausted, giving each other a peck on the cheek. Alice regularly transforms into the Blue Fairy, a doctor, Sleeping Beauty, and more and more often Cinderella, the one after the ball. The children are excited to see her, smiling and reaching out for her at any time of the day or night; they don't sleep, complain, throw temper tantrums on the floor, cry then laugh, then cry, never stop playing, and are obsessed with eating. She takes them to the pediatrician, dentist, ophthalmologist, orthodontist, psychologist, and physiotherapist, to the emergency room when Alexandre splits open his eyebrow or Émilie breaks her arm, along with their swimming classes, violin and piano lessons, judo and drama clubs, birthday parties for friends and family, and other parties. She goes to the parent-teacher meetings and for coffee with other mothers; she's the one who takes them to nursery and picks them up, to kindergarten, primary school, high school, the music conservatoire. When the weather's good on a Sunday, they all go to the Jardin du Luxembourg together with the stroller, bicycle, scooter, and boat. Jules has taken up running, Alice sits on a bench alone, watching the children, fascinated. When he was small, Alexandre liked to play with the stones, a few bits of wood, and pieces of string; he would build houses, towers, and sometimes even entire villages. He would spend hours playing with his wooden Kapla, his favorite game. Émilie preferred the swings, carousels, and puppet shows.

On Saturdays, Auntie Josette, Maurice, his wife Sandra and their children, Paul and his wife, and Jo, who is on his own and often depressed, come round. On Thursday evenings, Jules plays bridge with his friends while Alice minds the children, tells them stories, and gets them to do their homework. She didn't think she would blossom this well with motherhood, to the point where she would forget she is a woman and lose all interest in anything else. She writes her articles at night, submits them in the early hours, just before the deadline, and arrives at the office later and later. And Jules didn't think he'd be as happy as a father, or as happy not to be when he leaves home and finds some peace and quiet, far away from the tantrums, shouting, laughing, and crying. He delegates the children's upbringing to his wife, their homework, school, playtime, and even their punishments because, in principle and thanks to his character, he doesn't have any authority over them.

"We should think about buying a house in the countryside," Jules says.

"What for?"

"For weekends, for vacations . . . I can't stand Paris anymore. It's become too dark, too gray, too stressful. I feel like I spend my life on the metro. Look . . . a house beside the wild ocean, part of the landscape by the sea."

"Why not?"

"I visited a place near La Rochelle. There aren't many people there, it's not expensive. We could try to visit a plot of land. What do you think? The light there is fantastic. I can picture straight neat lines, a big bay window looking out over the ocean . . ."

"Jules . . . you haven't even asked me where I'd like to go. And you're suggesting somewhere no one ever goes."

"But . . . it's on the coast, a small town, well a village called Port-des-Barques. I went there for the multimedia library, remember?"

"Oh yes."

"There's a small square, a bakery, a church, fishermen's huts, a few pine trees. I'd really like to retire there."

"Have you lost your mind? Never in my life! In the deepest Charente . . . There's no way!"

"Maritime."

"What?"

"Charente-Maritime."

"It doesn't matter, Maritime or not. We'll die of boredom there. It's the kind of place that's desolate."

"Well, I'd like to build the house of my dreams by the ocean. It'll be like a cabin. Something simple and bright. We'll take long walks by the sea, on Île Madame. Our children will come, with our grandchildren. In the summer, we'll go swimming, and in the evening, we'll cozy up in front of the fire."

"What a nightmare! I'm never going there. Do you hear me?"

"So, where do you see us? When we're old?" he asks.

"I like Paris. I'll take walks every day in the Jardin du Luxembourg. I'll look at the trees, the statues, and the children playing with their little sailboats on the pond. I'll look at the trees; it'll remind me of my youth."

"I'll come too if I can see you through your cloud of pollution."

"Do you think we'll still love each other?" Alice asks.

"Yes."

"What makes you say that?"

"Let's play a game."

"Happy Families? Cluedo? Scrabble? Operation? Connect 4? Mr. Potato Head? Wait a minute until I get them."

"No, no, stop being silly. Do you remember the letter?"

"The letter you sent me when we first met?"

"Yes."

Alice looks at him, taken aback.

"I know it by heart. Would you like me to recite it for you?" she asks.

"Yes."

"What's gotten into you?"

She looks at him, suddenly struck. He looks at her with his blue eyes, staring into hers, serious and sad all of a sudden.

They sit like that for a few minutes. He carefully observes her long hair that frames her face, a few gray hairs showing, her forehead with a few fine lines across it, and the black rings under her dark eyes. His eyes well up.

"Are you crying?" she asks.

"No, no, I'm okay . . ."

"Tell me why you're crying . . ."

"I feel like we're growing apart, you and me. You know, Alice, that you're everything to me, don't you? I don't know what I'd be without you. And you know . . . if you were to ask me to throw myself out of the window, I'd do it."

"We live on the first floor, you idiot."

He comes closer and kisses her. She looks at him, not reacting, like he's doing something inappropriate, like she doesn't understand, even though they're lying in their bed. She's uncomfortable; she's not used to it anymore and doesn't want to. She gently pushes him away, takes the remote control to switch on the television, and they see the images of the Berlin Wall coming down, bit by bit.

"What was it like?" Jules asks. "You never told me."

"It was crazy, absolutely crazy," murmurs Alice. "No one could have predicted what happened over there."

"Paul was there too, with the embassy," Jules says. "Did you see him?"

Of course, she had seen him, Paul. But how could she tell Jules that? She would like to confess. She needs to tell someone everything, but she doesn't know who. Her heart soars. Arriving at the hotel, and this man whom she knows and recognizes, who she is happy to see here in this odd place, a tiny part of the free world, their giggles, wondering what they're doing there, if it's by chance, have you heard of serendipity? That "happy coincidence."

Did you follow me? Or was it a clever genie playing with our faint-heartedness? Which room were you in? The one just above mine? Or maybe the same one, due to a happy misunderstanding? Is there a word for this inexpressible concept? The wall that was coming down, brick by brick, smashed by a huge digger, the feeling of living through an important moment, a historical date. After leaving her things in her room, she went out and bumped into him again, talking away about an unbelievable event. They went to see for themselves, to the place where thousands of people from the East were crossing the border and escaping. He picked up a painted rock and gave it to her. They heard the words "*Unglaublich!*" The barrier had come down, and lines of cars were coming through, warmly welcomed by the Berliners. She is sitting cross-legged on the ground; he is beside her, strokes her face. It's cold; he puts his arms around her to warm her up. Her heart pounds, and her little transistor radio murmurs. There's music, a cello; it's the end of an era and the start of modernity, an era of freedom that triumphs with this human wave that flows in, these separated families who finally meet again, lines waiting to cross at Checkpoint Charlie, on both sides. Rostropovich gives an improvised concert at the wall—what more could he do in this moment? Suddenly they hear Bach, and everyone is moved, crying, laughing, shouting, some are drinking. With pickaxes, the Berliners destroy the border that separated them.

In the early hours, Alice and Paul return to the hotel together, and in a foregone conclusion that seems much easier to accept when you're far from home, as though it was natural, they sleep together. That night, all they do is sleep.

And that's the worst thing of all, thinks Alice as she turns off the light, happier than she has been in a long time.

9.
Paris, May 1981

A scream rips through the silence. Jules trembles all over. He looks at Alice, terrified. Her eyes bulging, sweat dripping from her brow, panting, she's screaming loud enough to burst her husband's eardrums as she digs her fingers into his arm, grabbing it, crushing it, twisting it painfully.

He tries to talk to her, tells her to try thinking of something nice, like a Joe Dassin slow number, *Été Indienne*, the one she loves, the one they danced to at parties, at "blasts," in clubs. He sings, "We shall go wherever you wish, whenever you want, and we'll still love each other even when love is dead?" It makes her smile and even break into an absurd laugh in the midst of the pain.

What does that even mean, "When summer is gone?" Those lyrics don't make any sense, she thinks. Then her mind wanders to the Castel in Rue Princess in Saint-Germain-des-Prés in Paris that replaced the jazz clubs she liked to go to when she was younger. Before Alexandre was born, they drank, partied, laughed, and went home at six in the morning after dancing all night. Jules still goes there with Paul; he feels good there, free, happy, and "alive." When he slinks back into that establishment with its red velvet and tiptoes stealthily up the stairs or goes down into the basement, passing Serge Gainsbourg, Jacques Dutronc, and Françoise Hardy, pretty boys, yé-yé singers, disco dancers, and rockers, he feels like he's been reborn.

All of a sudden, another wave of contractions comes, and the pain is so excruciating that Alice can't believe she had forgotten it after the last time. She's mad at herself for having started over and repeated this mistake after swearing she would never put herself through it again when Alexandre was born. The pain of the contractions, the tearing as he came out, the hemorrhoids and chafing, the lactation, blockages, and stomachaches that had become her daily fate, she who not so long ago had been a warrior, a woman in a Rodier twinset who got things done, who could crisscross France in her Fiat Panda to get that story. Since then, she's seen forceps, had an episiotomy that damaged her perineum, got fed up with the physio exercises she was prescribed to avoid incontinence when she sneezes or laughs, and become a slave to her son, day and night, this tiny, greedy little tyrant who doesn't give her the time to breathe and for whom she would do anything.

The first time, with Alexandre, she had realized that something significant was about to happen but didn't know what it was exactly. She couldn't find a way to break the news to Jules, and she had been anxious. When she had come home to their small one-bedroom apartment after the blood test and he asked her about the results, she had replied, "Nothing." As she had said the word, she turned red, trembled, gone weak, and almost confessed everything, like she'd done something wrong, committed a crime, broken the law, like it was a disgrace. Of course, there was something. She was so unsettled that she had preferred not to think about it. Pregnant—afraid she was, and afraid that she might not be anymore. She had read in a magazine that you shouldn't say anything for the first three months because so many pregnancies end in miscarriage.

Another contraction starts, pinning her to the bed. She doesn't even have the strength to scream anymore. She hangs on, stiff, winded. Utter madness. She never should have done it. She regrets it now. Why did she want this baby so much? When she had heard she was pregnant, she had been a little surprised because she was over forty and really hadn't expected it anymore. She was proud and worried, happy and sad, surprised and terrified. When she had told Jules in the Jardin du Luxembourg, he hadn't taken it well. Surprised and thrown off balance, like he had been crushed by responsibility, he had hesitated before hugging her and saying he was happy. He had actually looked at her as though he was devastated. When they had got home, he had done the sums to work out a potential budget for the year ahead. Did they really have enough to live on with two children? She wrote articles for newspapers but didn't have a permanent job, and he had gotten into debt to start his architectural firm and buy a car.

The doctor comes into the delivery room with the midwife, a young woman with a white scrub tunic and a white face. She doesn't recognize him and thinks that her mind is going, but he introduces himself and tells her he is replacing the obstetrician who is on vacation. *Is that his real name, or is it a joke?* Alice wonders when she sees the name on his green uniform, Dr. Risk. They both busy themselves between the widespread legs of the woman giving birth who has done everything she can to expel this child but isn't succeeding. Screams come from the room next door.

"Kill me! I can't take it anymore . . . Kill me! I beg you!"

Another woman is giving birth. The obstetrician leaves the room in a hurry to go and see what is happening. It has gone quiet; she's silent, or at any rate, no longer has the strength to shout. Or perhaps she has been silenced, finished off by Dr. Risk?

Alice clings to Jules so tightly that he starts to scream, too, because she has drawn blood. She looks at him, lost, and he half-smiles. Is it a girl or a boy? Who will it look like? What if it looks like Jo, with his boxer's jaw and crooked nose?

After a moment of respite, the spasms start again, increasing in intensity. It's excruciating; she loses her mind and is going to faint. The monitor panics, and Jules, too. The baby is in distress; the midwife calls the doctor in, assists him, and to avoid taking any risks, he starts to slice. He cuts her!

And finally, the child appears. It's there, on Alice, on her belly, at her breast. A distraught baby, stunned, exhausted, terrified from the effort and the fight, just like its mother. It is a tiny little girl, 5 lbs, 4 ounces, who opens her mouth for her first cry, covered in wax, blood, and amniotic fluid. She starts to wail, shrill shrieks, regular and weak.

Dr. Risk cuts the umbilical cord and frees the baby, placing her in her mother's arms, and she smiles in tears.

"Help me sew her up, Sylvia," Dr. Risk instructs the midwife.

Jules looks at her, terrified, and wonders why he agreed to attend this carnage when, with Alexandre, he had waited at the cafe around the corner, drinking a beer with Paul. He turns pale, his legs give way, and he is caught by the midwife while the doctor takes care of Alice. But she can't feel anything anymore, is in a daze, and is about to pass out. Alice, torn apart and stitched back together. Pale Alice, with this child in a hospital room, is crushed and exhausted. At the same time, the baby screams even louder despite being so small. Alice gives her the breast that she miraculously begins to suckle as if she already knew how—determined, grateful, and finally pacified. She opens her eyes without seeing her mother, breathes in her smell, and falls asleep against her, with her eyes rolled back in her head and not a word of thanks.

Jules takes the baby as it yawns in bliss, with one of those reflex smiles that suddenly light up the faces of newborns who don't even see the person they're looking at, an automatic smile that covers every expression, astonishment, sadness, anger, surprise, disgust, and that unbelievable ability to see every living being and thing with an insatiable curiosity.

As Alice dozes, Jules turns on the television in the hospital room to watch the election results. Pixel by pixel, the face of the new president is revealed, to everyone's surprise. Seeing François Mitterrand's face appear a few hours after that of his daughter, Jules literally leaps for joy. Swept up by his campaign dreams, he's exhilarated, transfigured by joy and a sense of revolution in this unique moment in his life. We won, he shouts. We won!

Alice, at the sound of this news, wakes up and starts to sob.

"Why are you crying, Alice?"

"I'm thinking about the pregnant women who were deported . . . I can't stand the idea."

"But why? Why now?"

"How can you not think about it?"

Alice struggles to celebrate like Jules, who grabs the phone to call all his friends, full of excitement and overjoyed.

Engulfed by morbid thoughts, she suddenly pictures herself jumping out of the window with her baby that she anxiously examines, and a terrible sense of guilt, regret, and dread even overwhelms her.

"Jules," murmurs Alice.

"What's wrong?"

"I can't just sit here."

"What?"

"I'm fat, torn, my bladder is leaking, and I've got hemorrhoids."

"Something has to be done, Alice."

"What?"

"A regime."

"That's not it, that's not the problem."

"What's the problem, then?"

"I'm the problem. I'm sad, Jules. So sad."

Sitting on the bed, listless, unable to move or say a word, Alice can't stop sobbing, thinking to herself that she couldn't possibly be less happy. Jules takes her hand, gently caresses her face, tries to talk to her, reassure her, but he feels like something is beyond his reach, that he can't change anything for her, apart from trying to distract her with Mitterrand's election, with everything about this happy event that will change society, change things for them. He tells her he has met some people, new friends, who asked him to join their group, well, their lodge, actually. She looks at him, not understanding what he's saying, what the connection with the happy event is, so he tells her he loves her, that he's overjoyed at having a child with her, a second child, a daughter, an enchanting, sweet little princess who will have deep, dark eyes, and who will reign over his heart, who will always be there for him, and he will be there for her, like a renewed promise, a pledge of love, a love that lasts. Isn't that true, my love?

"What shall we call her?" Jules asks.

"Clara," Alice says, forcing herself to smile, eyes teary, "like my mother."

"Why not Émilie?"

"No," Alice says. "She'll be Clara. I always wanted a little Clara."

"As you wish, darling," Jules says. "You're the one who decides."

10.

Paris, May 1968

Long hair, light blue eyes, fixed grin, determined and wild-looking, Jules is wearing jeans, a colorful shirt, and his suede jacket as he goes out to join the student riots in the Latin Quarter. He meets his dear friend Paul from Nice. An active member of the national student's union, the UNEF, and the French Unified Socialist Party, the PSU, Jules admires Jean-Paul Sartre for his commitment and support for the rebellion and has also joined the Trotskyist movement in the French Revolutionary Communist Youth, the JCR. He spends a lot of time at gatherings, meetings, and general assemblies. He's determined to do away with the bourgeoisie and its patriarchal values, authoritarian and deeply unjust, and to never get bogged down in the traditional family model, just like Jean-Paul Sartre and Simone de Beauvoir, who reject the concept of the couple and remain open to any propositions or opportunities that arise, on pain of alienating that which they hold most dear, the only thing they do not possess, freedom.

Together, Jules and Paul slice their way through the

crowd to Place Denfert-Rochereau, where the Lion of Belfort reigns over the square, seated on its four paws above the brawl, looking toward the Statue of Liberty to proclaim its power. They shout at the top of their lungs how much they hate the government, are in solidarity with those on strike who signed Daniel Cohn-Bendit's Manifesto of the 142 against American imperialism, who besieged and occupied Nanterre, emptied a trashcan over a professor's head, and defied the police. Facing the riot squad, a crowd of ten thousand now wants to free the Sorbonne. In the mass, Jules and Paul meet two young women with long, straight hair wearing miniskirts, leather boots, and pretty smiles. One is called Stéphanie, and the other is Marie-Claude. They drag them along and melt into the group of students, high schoolers, and anyone who wants to change society and sing the *Internationale* at the top of their lungs. For them, tonight is the revolution.

Alice is late—a cylinder head blew on her 2CV, and she ends up stranded on the roadside. She eventually abandons her car, which has definitely seen it all: adventures at Café de Flore or the Deux Magots, demonstrations, feminist gatherings, and meetings, wild adventures inland, and weekends by the sea in Cabourg and Deauville. She, too, has been swept up by the air of freedom in the city and on the angry streets at the dawn of new births, promises, and revivals. She walks toward the Latin Quarter to try and find Jules. She has read *Memoirs of a Dutiful Daughter* and *The Second Sex*, which opened her eyes to male domination and the violence of the patriarchy. A suffocating society where women do the chores, cook, and take care of the children—where they are beaten, exploited, stolen, and raped. She has no intention whatsoever of living a life devoted to her husband and children; she's hungry for action and activism and has started writing pamphlets, articles, and news reports for several left-wing newspapers. That's why she's in a hurry to join the women's march today, with its banners and slogans. They want to break out of their prison, the fetters of their upbringing, and build independent lives—an existence, to use a popular turn of phrase.

Alice stops at the Café de Flore, where she is supposed to meet Jules. But while she waits, she sees another man arrive, with long hair, wearing a jacket and jeans, and a disarming smile. He's so handsome, with his dark eyes and stubble. He gives her a kiss and whispers in her ear, "And who are you, *mademoiselle*?" Bewildered, she doesn't know what to say, so they smile at each other just as Jules arrives and introduces the young man to Alice. It's his friend Paul, who was with him in Algeria, and he is from Nice. Paul, you know? I've told you a lot about him. Oh yes, Paul . . . Hi, I'm Alice, Jules' wife?

Suddenly swept up by the crowd, the shouts, the hysteria, all three of them are carried along to the Santé Prison to support the students from Nanterre who were locked up after occupying the Sorbonne on May 3rd, and they shout in unison: Free our comrades!

But Alice loses sight of them, caught up, despite herself, in a swarm of students heading toward Boulevard

Saint-Germain. Some leave, others stay, and more arrive as they reach the Latin Quarter. Some are looking for violence, and others want to talk. Some are looking to fight, and others are looking to negotiate. Some are looking for revolution, and others are supporting them. They take planks from building sites, cardboard boxes, and anything they can get their hands on to build barricades. Rue Saint-Jacques, Rue Royer-Collard, Rue des Irlandais, Rue Gay-Lussac. Some of them are six and a half feet tall; the area is walled-in. The students face off against the police, the riot squads, and the mobile teams set up in 1944, forty units dispatched simultaneously across Paris to quash the riots. At their end, Paul and Jules move away from the street fights that they don't like, which remind them of the war. They have fled the riot police armed with clubs, tear gas, and shields to join the students equipped only with their slogans. They look for Alice but don't find her: She has met feminist comrades and an informal group led by a young female activist. The woman urges them to live in plain sight, not closed off in a homosexual ghetto, and is thinking about starting a radical movement to protest against the patriarchy, inspired by the American sisterhoods. She tells Alice that heterosexual women can love women too and could consider becoming lesbians as a political choice.

It is midnight at the barricades, but no one feels like going home. Jules and Paul have found Marie-Claude and Stéphanie again, and they have gotten involved in the fight against the riot squads who have started to attack. At 2 o'clock in the morning, they sweep Rue Auguste-Comte and Boulevard Saint-Michel, wreck the barricades, and lob tear gas grenades at the students who retaliate with cobblestones, shouting, "CRS-SS" and "De Gaulle, killer!" and setting fire to everything they find—cars and barricades. As the police move forward, the number of casualties increases. Jules, Paul, and the girls, caught up in the action and energy of the crowd, run, escape, split up, lose each other, find each other again, lose each other again, and finally meet up again.

Alice and the young feminist leave the group of students; they flee the petrol bombs and run to the one-bedroom apartment where Alice lives with Jules, in the heart of the Latin Quarter. They drink a bottle of vodka, smoke some hash, and use anything they can to toast the revolution. They drink and smoke; their hands touch, first one, then the other; their heads move closer; they swoon; they slip away from their own story, from history, from time. They're light and hazy. Their bodies seek each other and come together. Their skin finds pleasure and melts; their flesh merges. They don't let go, like they're attempting the impossible—and carried away by the frenzy of the night, they give themselves up to their ecstasy.

That morning, Paris awakes in a moment of grace, undoubtedly the reason this instant is so beautiful, set in the middle of nowhere, like a landmark, a punctuation mark, a new start without a tomorrow. The woman from the night before gets up, collects her things, and, before leaving, retraces her steps to leave a souvenir, a parting gift. While Alice is still sleeping, without her seeing but hoping she'll find it later, the woman discretely leaves a book in the bookcase. A volume by a young Czech writer. On the flyleaf, she has added a short dedication: *In memory of this crazy night, S.*

11.

May 1962

The spouses shall show each other all due respect, fidelity, succor, and assistance.

Alice and Jules swear eternal love for each other in the large, wooden-paneled room in the city hall. Full of grace, she wears her pearled finery, trimmed with lace and open-backed, a rigid corset highlighting her waist, and under her décolleté, shown off by the fine straps, her heart pounds. Jules is wearing a gray suit with a vest and a blue tie, as well as a side parting like Cary Grant in *North by Northwest*. They are young, beautiful, overwhelmed, and finally happy after waiting seven years, but no second thoughts, just the twists of life and war, commitments made and broken, the tribulations of life. They are happy, awestruck, and overawed when the mayor pronounces the sentence that unites them through the holy bond of marriage, along with the articles of the civil code: *Spouses shall jointly provide moral and material support to the family and contribute to maintaining it. They shall provide for the upbringing of children and prepare for their future. Where a marital agree-*

ment does not regulate the contribution of the spouses to the household expenses, they shall contribute to such expenses in proportion to their respective abilities. The spouses undertake to live together maritally.

On one side, Jules' family, his father, his brother, his sister-in-law, his grandparents, his uncles, aunts, and cousins, and on Alice's side, Auntie Josette and a few friends. Two destinies unite, look at each other, smile at each other, complement each other, and greet each other politely. Solemnly, Jules slips the ring onto Alice's finger as she looks at him, tears in her eyes; he holds her face in his hands to kiss her with tenderness, passion, and devotion. Then, their witnesses, Jules' brother Maurice and Auntie Josette, sign the marriage certificate. Just before the wedding, Auntie Josette had given Alice a carefully wrapped package that she wasn't too open until she had returned home.

"It was your mother's," she whispers.

Later in the afternoon, the celebrations continue in an ornate room in the Grand Hotel overlooking the sea. Jules purses his lips to hold back his tears. Alice smiles, swept up by joy, swirls, and dances in her white silk dress with Auntie Josette, who is shaded by a cream hat that matches her elegant suit.

During the religious ceremony that follows the civil ceremony, the Rabbi unites Jules and Alice through the holy bonds of marriage a second time. And Jules slips the ring onto Alice's finger, saying with this ring, you are mine. An orchestra plays Yiddish music, and a violin soars in an infinitely sad melody that pierces the soul and delights the heart. Outside on the terrace, the weather is good; the atmosphere is gay; the air is warm; the faces are full of smiles, tears, and complicity; and hearts are burning. Jo dances with Auntie Josette, Maurice with all the women there and even with the grandparents who have traveled for the occasion. Tears in his eyes, Jules walks over to Alexandre and Émilie, emotional, and cups their gaunt faces, ridged with marks and wrinkles, the beautiful faces of his ancestors, and kisses them gently. All that is left is love, which, for them, came in the form of sacrifice, devotion, and regard for nothing but their well-being and survival in everyday life.

Then Jules gets up and walks to the middle of the room. In front of everyone, including Alice, who is watching him, clearly moved, he begins his speech.

"Dear friends, thank you for joining us. Thank you to my very dear grandparents, Alexandre and Émilie Gardot. Thanks to you, I had a childhood. There is only one thing I wish for tonight: that Alice and I may remain as united as you are. I would also like to thank my father, Joseph, and my brother, Maurice, for always being there for me. I remember our mother, too. She is always with me. We know what you went through during the war. I would like to thank my father, who, along with Maman and the other members of the immigrant workers union, the MOI, arranged for Jewish children to flee to Switzerland. I shall always—until I take my last breath—remember that time when we were on the road with our suitcases, silver coins sewn into the linings of our coats, and when we arrived in that village in Isère. And every day, I'm filled with pride, knowing that I have had parents like you, and I hope I am worthy of being your son. For as long as I live, I shall always remember Maman, who paid with her life for her heroic actions and generosity in the face of barbarity.

"I also feel deep affection for my parents-in-law, who are not here this evening. Alice, I know that you're thinking of them too and that we both miss them terribly today. So I would simply like to say that I would like to thank them too, wherever they may be, for having given me Alice. For having saved her too, on that day, on July 16, 1942, when she was only a young girl and the only thing they could do was leave her with a neighbor so she could survive.

"And that neighbor is Josette—Auntie Josette—who took Alice in and hid her. We know what you did because you saved the lives of other Jewish children who were left on their own after their parents were arrested, and that you did so risking your own life, too. That is why we shall always call you Auntie Josette, like all the children you saved.

"I won't thank everyone who traveled to get here, long distances even . . . from Spain, Italy, America. It's crazy to think what some people will do to get a free meal these days! But more seriously, friends . . . there is one thing I would like to say. Or rather I would like to read to you because I have prepared a short text.

"Alice, darling.

"We met at a wedding. It was by chance, yet it was not by chance since we had every chance of meeting eventually at our mutual friends' home.

"We recognized each other, talked, argued, and like a shooting star, you disappeared, leaving a waft of unforgettable fragrance behind you.

"Because Alice . . . that's your name, isn't it? You are everything to me, and I would give everything for you. If you were to ask me to throw myself into the North Sea, I would do it immediately. But I'd prefer the Mediterranean because it's warmer, and that's where we're flying to tomorrow . . ."

That night, in a beautiful room overlooking the sea in the Grand Hotel in Cabourg, Jules draws near to his wife, embraces her, looks at her, and caresses her. He talks to her about love, her face, her eyes, her mouth, what they express, and everything he feels for her.

Finally, they discover each other, their unwavering, burning flesh warming each other in an embrace that is theirs alone, that they create together, with their hands, their hearts, their gaze, a sweet, intense mix of tenderness, strength, and emotion. The way they connect and absorb each other transforms them. With their movements, they express their love for each other. Jules' hands run over Alice's body, examining it, sculpting it. They make love, and love makes them. From time to time, their eyes wander to look at the horizon or contemplate some unknown faraway memory. They cannot resist: Their desire commands. "Are you okay?" he asks. That question, are you okay . . .

Outside, the sea extends like a sheet of blue steel, cold and distant. The first light of dawn illuminates it without warming it. The horizon gradually emerges, like an impervious background ready to unfold when the light shines on the world and on the town, this small town of Cabourg, romantic and old-fashioned, where they decided to celebrate their marriage. In the distance, on the blue line of the horizon, liners arrive, in succession, to deliver their cargo to the port of Le Havre. It's like a dream, seeing them slowly return from their long, unknown voyage.

The next day, they fly to Naples, check into a small hotel in the center, and walk down the streets and along the wide avenues, hand in hand. Then they take the boat to Capri and arrive on the south side of the island with its squares and beaches. The town built into the rocks on a promontory dominates the horizon with its gardens and small, whitewashed, one-story houses. A motorboat carries them to the Blue Grotto, where the color of the sea is like nothing they've ever seen before. In the evening, as the sun sets, sitting across from each other, they look at each other and confide in each other. She doesn't want to talk about her childhood anymore. It's like her life starts with him, this very instant, in this village with colored houses lining the harbor, with its alleyways, boutiques, and cafes.

When they return, Jules and Alice move into their small, 320-square-foot, one-bedroom apartment on the third floor of a block in Rue Mouffetard in the heart of the Latin

Quarter. It is empty but seems vast to them. It needs to be furnished, inhabited, and decorated. The young bride finally opens the gift from Josette: a pretty Art Deco lamp made of pewter and white glass that she carefully sets on a small table, taking every precaution possible. It's the first object they place in their home, and she has tears in her eyes: It's the only thing she has that belonged to her parents.

They gradually settle in. Jules is studying architecture and works as a school monitor, a ticket inspector on the metro, and a night watchman. He comes home at dawn, tired, just as Alice wakes up to go to class. They buy their clothes at Barbès—sweaters, pants, skirts, and duffle coats. She does the grocery shopping and cooks—simple meals. She doesn't spend too much time in the kitchen and isn't as interested in earthly nourishment as she is in spiritual nourishment. They go to the college refectory at lunchtime where they have pasta. It's easier and not expensive; it's cheaper, in fact.

They study for their degrees and go to class. In the summer, they revise for their exams. They aren't planning to have a child: They are big children themselves caught up in their own torment. Gripped by anxiety, she wakes up at night, suffering from insomnia. Often terrified by crowds, by the thought of going out, meeting people. He, on the other hand, is sociable, on the lookout, is sometimes depressed, sometimes funny, happy, full-on, handsome, morose, with those eyes of his, one serious, the other joyful, the two sides to his personality. He can dance, sing, and tell stories but is also susceptible to morbid, suicidal thoughts at the slightest headache or stomachache.

They build their life together, walking along the Seine, around Montmartre, to the places where he grew up. Jules always has something to do, something on the go, sports, an exhibition, a walk. He loves swimming and takes Alice to the pool in Rue Blomet, which he admires for its architecture. With the money he has earned, he buys a small, white Peugeot 404 they use to explore the area around Paris, the Chevreuse valley, the Eure forests, going as far as Normandy. They like to leave on a Sunday morning and go to Cabourg to drink a coffee at the beach. Jules has discovered a passion for decorating; he hunts for bargains at the Saint-Ouen flea market and barters for old furniture to liven up their apartment. He even bought himself a suede jacket that Alice likes a lot. They often go for dinner with Jules' brother and his fiancée. Alice is happy to have found a family beyond Auntie Josette. Jules forgets Alice's birthday, but it doesn't matter. Their tiny bathroom even serves as an office when they need some time alone. Jules has bought a television and watches *Intervilles*, the new comedy game show presented by Guy Lux, Léon Zitrone, and Simone Garnier. On Thursdays, he plays bridge, rummy, and poker with his brother and friends while Alice works at home.

Jules and Alice love spending hours talking about everything and nothing. Alice greatly admires her husband, his visionary nature, his culture, creativity, and generosity. Madly in love with her, he watches her from morning to night. He loves how she is both determined and shy, cultured and curious, strong and sensitive. With her long brown hair that she straightens or curls as she wishes with multicolored rollers, her dark eyes adorned with fake lashes, her small mouth with straight teeth, freckles on her slightly snub nose, her willowy silhouette and slim legs, she is the very essence of the feminine ideal for him.

They go to the cinema, watch *Lawrence of Arabia* twice in a row, wander around Saint-Germain, drink coffee at the Café de Flore or the Deux Magots, and watch the passersby, cars, Parisian life that is coming alive with a lease of new life, a wind of hope. Women in miniskirts and sweaters, young and old, lovers holding hands, kissing in the street. And in the evenings, they go to the Castel with friends, the new club on Rue Princess, in a three-story block, where they bump into Jean-Pierre Cassel, Françoise Dorléac, Brigitte Bardot, and Régine and Françoise Sagan. They dance the twist, jazz, and the java until midnight. They come home in the early hours and make love to a Serge Gainsbourg record. Effusively, tenderly, passionately, they come close, unite, wanting each other more and more, never satisfied. They are swept up by the desire that connects their bodies and their minds. And with his words, he enchants her, charms her, seduces her, wants to melt into her, and she wants to become one with him, for them to be joined. They are alone in the world like nothing else exists and like nothing else is important beyond the entanglement of their bodies that disappear and meet, seek each other, and miss each other. The more he looks at her, the more he desires her. And she is deeply moved to feel him so close to her. She believes their destinies are connected, forever, and that nothing shall ever separate them. And he, through her, tries to indulge in life, to lose his memory, and forget his nightmares, those troubling images from the past that still haunt him.

12.

Aïn-Sefra, Algeria, 1957

"It's a war," Jules says, "but the enemy is invisible. Assaults everywhere, attacks, civilians massacred. Explosions in the cities, bullets from every direction. It's actually a war against the population."

"What are they doing?"

"They torture and kill. Europeans are being slaughtered in the streets, too; bombs are exploding. And they call them 'events.' The government isn't doing anything. Guy Mollet is letting himself be intimidated by protestors; he's influenced by ministers living in Algiers. Robert Lacoste calls for the tough method. In short, everyone lets the authorities and military take action. I feel like I'm part of an unjust war, that I'm on the wrong side. The colonists say they developed the country and pushed back the lions, yet the way they treat the Algerians in the name of their ideology is despicable. And then there are the dead, the thousands who have been killed. They tell us that the French have been in Algeria for over a hundred years, that it's a French province, so it's a civil war, fratricide, lots of them want to stay French. But at night . . . I block my ears so I don't hear the screams in the casbahs."

Alice listens to Jules, moved at hearing him on the telephone. The last time she saw him, they were sitting on a bench in the Jardin du Luxembourg. That's where they meet, where they spend afternoons together, in an embrace, kissing, drawn to each other like magnets. Then Jules was called up and integrated into the platoon of gunmen on tanks in La Valbonne, near Lyon, in the 8th regiment of cuirassiers, and transferred to Algeria. They parted heartbroken, promising to write to each other and to talk as often as possible.

Since Jules left, Alice has gone on pilgrimages to the places where they spent time together: cafés, the banks of the Seine, restaurants, and narrow streets rather than main roads. Misty bridges in the early hours, avenues with stunning window displays, attic rooms still lit up where students labored over their essays, the paths along the riverside with the green stands the booksellers keep under lock and key, and Place de la Concorde in the evening, under the drizzle, lit up by long lines of streetlamps.

In his letters, Jules describes the lunar landscape, rocky and sandy, in the Ksour Mountains, at an altitude of more than 1,000 meters. He tells her about life at the military post that guarantees security at the start of the Sahara. Since his promotion to second lieutenant, he is in command of a platoon in an even more isolated area near an

Arab village where nothing happens. The desert: an absurd life in the heat, faced with oneself and with the wind. The sandstorms, when the horizon suddenly darkens, and you have only a few minutes to take shelter. And the beauty of the empty beaches, where the soldiers are allowed to go on a three-day leave. They swim, enjoying the brief moment of respite when time stands still. He tells her about the sirocco that drives men mad. Their mission is to "maintain the position." Thankfully, he has a transistor to help fill the loneliness at night. He listens to Europe No. 1; it saves him from his captain's madness, who, to galvanize the troops, tells them they are part of an army "like no other," an elite army in which one must be impeccable with a perfectly ironed uniform, perfect hair, well turned out.

He also mentions another man he has met, a soldier with whom he gets on well because they share the same views. He's from Nice and grew up in a left-wing family. During many long evenings, they wonder why they are there. They share their ideas and ideals, become richer through their dreams, and inhale them like fresh air in order to bear the asphyxiating war. Jules talks to him for hours about Alice and even reads him his letters, the ones he writes her almost every day, and the ones he receives.

"And how are you, my darling?" Jules asks on the telephone.

"Oh, nothing new. I'm just trying to understand."

"Understand what?"

"Where I'm from."

"Where are you from, Alice? I wonder that, too."

"Honestly. I'd like to know more about my family, about my past. I found a trace of my grandfather thanks to a letter he sent from Dachau. It unsettled me when I read it. He said he was going to come back, that they would be freed. And then they didn't hear from him again. Do you think I'll find out what happened to him one day?"

"I hope so, I truly do, Alice."

"I barely knew my parents. I don't have any brothers or sisters. Just Josette. It's like I never had any family at all."

"Then I shall be your family."

Alice likes hearing his voice. She is soothed by his words. She could spend hours hanging onto the telephone listening to him talk, but they are often interrupted. At night, when she struggles to fall asleep, she sometimes reads the letter that Jules wrote her just after they met. The letter that she cherishes even more now he is absent, in which he tells her everything. She reads it and breathes it to fill the gap and absence that drive her to distraction.

Two months later, with *Black and Blue* by Sidney Bechet playing in the background, Jules and Alice meet again in a bar in Saint-Germain, happy to finally see each other again. They order gin and tonics, whisper in each other's ear, smile at each other, brush against each other, touching, because the music is so loud, so enticing, they can't take their eyes off each other, paying attention to every little detail. Jules has swapped his uniform for a gray suit. His hair is thick, almost cropped, which makes his blue eyes and soft smile stand out even more, but his expression is dark-er now. The young man, barely more than an adolescent when she last saw him, has given way to a man who is thinner, emaciated, and aged before his time. His face emanates a sense of fatality, fatigue and suffering, worry too. And the desire to live each moment as though it were the last. Alice is wearing a bright red twin-set and a pencil skirt wrapped around her long, slim legs on high heels. She has tamed her hair into a pretty chignon, put on some mascara and pink lipstick to highlight her smile and perfect, pearly teeth, and has hidden her freckles under a layer of foundation.

Jules takes Alice's hand, leads her to the dance floor, and they dance. The rhythm is slow, and their bodies meet. They embrace and kiss amidst the smoke, alcohol, and laughter around them, to the sound of the musicians improvising until late into the night. They become dizzy and lightheaded; the jazz knocks them over, foils their expectations, and pushes them to cling to each other. She quivers with happiness and desire.

Then, much later, a little tipsy, they go out into the cold night, wrapped up in their coats, try to hail a taxi, then another, but can't get one to stop at this hour. Everyone is rushing out into the streets while horns sound, so they walk in the icy wind, their breath making white plumes, two silhouettes that flee into the night, fugitives with nowhere to go apart from the city in the early hours, life. She smiles at him, and with that smile, she tells him that the most important thing is what is happening between us, here and now; nothing else matters, the past, the war, the mistakes, the regrets, the expectations. This encounter, between us. This desire to know each other, see each other again, be together. Who can stop it? It's more than natural; it's urgent. And already the fear of losing each other. They have to tell each other everything before they separate again when dawn breaks.

They are so happy they want to savor each moment; they don't have the right to be together. Their union, illicit, is deemed an offense to decency, and to put it plainly, adultery, a criminal offense punishable with a court sentence. They meet in the greatest secrecy—because Jules is married.

13.
Paris, 9 May 1955

"I declare you husband and wife."

The mayor reads out the articles of the Civil Code. The bride is beautiful, her head held high, her hazelnut brown eyes, and a bright smile. She has a bouquet of white flowers in her hands, pale like her, set in green, a combination that suggests purity and springtime. It's moving and joyful, crazy and a little funny, because it's always the same, this ceremony that everyone has seen since childhood and which one attends with wonder. The couple that are joined in this moment look at each other. She half-smiles, and he holds back a tear. Embarrassed, shy, and happy, they burst out laughing, candid, victorious: There they are, husband and wife.

She had met this young man who would become her husband at a friends' party. They courted, and she introduced him to her parents, industrialists who live in the XVIth arrondissement in Paris. The situation had to be made official quickly. Plan the wedding, move into an apartment chosen by the father, settle in, find a profession, and start his life. Thérèse, twenty-three, didn't want to work; she wished to devote herself to her home and husband. Her mother gave her the *Good Housewife's Guide*, according to which one must always be cheerful and interesting, must tidy and clean one's home to make sure it is comfortable and serene, make sure that the dinner is ready when one's spouse comes home, avoid making noise with, for example, the vacuum cleaner or other household appliances, when he is resting, listen to him, let him speak first, never complain, and yield to his every desire.

But just as the husband in question prepares to sign the marriage certificate, he looks up and sees, astonished, a woman with long straight hair, a mischievous glint in her eyes, freckles on her thin, perfect nose, smiling, charming, and happy. It's her, there's no doubt—the young woman he had bumped into the day before in the Jardin du Luxembourg. He hesitates, looks at her again, then signs the certificate. *Jules Gardot*.

He promises to never look up at her again, but it's impossible. The more he tries not to, the more he does. Their bodies speak a silent, indiscernible language that only they can hear. Their souls search for each other. They begin a secret, passionate dialogue. It is as if another dimension has opened up; all of a sudden, another life lurks in the lulls of their lives. A pure presence where two empty shells are filled, each by the other. The lost beings search for and find each other through a mystical movement. All of a sudden, they are hurt by their lack of consistency, for not having been themselves, but rather prisoners of convention, of society, of their faint-heartedness. The ground opens up beneath their feet, and the sky above their heads is torn open. In a flash, it makes them dizzy. As though bewitched, they teeter, heads spinning. A thrill takes hold of them, grabs them, and silences them.

So they greet each other with a brief exchange and a glance that lingers, shows interest, leaves, and returns. A glance that makes their hearts quiver as their bodies are drawn to each other. He is tall and slim; his eyes stare deep into hers. She has brown hair, her eyelids shimmer with blue eye shadow, and her red lips murmur, "Hello . . . I'm Alice . . . Thérèse's friend." "And I'm Jules, Thérèse's husband."

"I'm afraid, Jules, that you've lost your way here, in this town hall, on this beautiful May Day."

"What place does love have in your life?" he asks.

"Have you ever caught the eye of anyone who has moved you so deeply?"

"Yes, yesterday, I believe, in the Jardin du Luxembourg. Or perhaps in another life."

The sentences they hear are only in their imagination as the orchestra plays jazz.

Alice shouldn't have been there. She had arrived at the ceremony late in her green 2CV, a small box on four wheels that had stalled in the middle of the road but had eventually started again, sputtering.

Jules shouldn't have been there either but for other reasons. Because he had let himself be carried along by life, because he was a young man who had been brought up well, decent, who did not go out with a woman without marrying her. Because that was how he had been brought up by his parents and his grandparents.

And here Jules is, signing his name, with Alice watching him, wanting to flee, afraid her car would turn into a real pumpkin.

After the town hall, there is a reception at a restaurant in the middle of the Bois de Boulogne. The tables are decorated with white and pink flowers. Jules can't help but notice Alice's presence, and she can't bring herself to look up without catching Jules' eye. And in those glances, it is clear that they are both destined for each other, even though they are not entirely aware of it yet, though they can't find the words to say it, even though, at this moment in time, they avert their gaze, embarrassed, surprised, restrained, afraid. And even if their eyes meet again, accidentally, linger, lock, to the extent that they feel perplexed, disturbed almost, and Jules would like to make a move in her direction, to invite her to dance before she's snatched away by someone else, and all he can see is her back, with her long hair that has come undone over the course of the evening, touching her shoulders, slight, and when, carried by the crowd, he loses sight of her, searches for her in vain in the melee, feverishly scanning the room to see where she is. But one never knows why these things happen, why someone touches your heart and soul, that one person and no one else, like a revelation that would be the final confession, since there is no other after all—or at least not one that you will meet in this earthly life.

She slips away without saying a word, without saying

goodbye, without leaving an address or phone number, not even a farewell. Jules walks around the lake alone in the middle of the Bois de Boulogne. It is dark and still at this late hour. He walks, or rather flies, *La Foule* by Edith Piaf, as played by the wedding band, still in his head. He stops at the water's edge where the boats are and sits down on a bench to look out at the lake and watch the moon sink into it like a huge sphere drowning. Mesmerized by the silver reflection, he lets himself be soothed by the lapping of the water. A gentle breeze caresses him and rustles the trees, their gentle shadows surrounding him, enveloping him in their dark cloak.

He is happy, intoxicated, drunk, and in love. Where is she from? Where is she going? What does she know? Does she know it's her?

He thinks about seeing her again, like a vestal virgin on a small boat sailing away from him, smiling, toward a mythical and mysterious horizon.

He thinks about his wife, waiting for him in the hotel, alone in her room. His wife, in her translucent dress, on their wedding night.

He thinks about the Breton writer he likes so much, Armand Robin, and the poem that he wrote, "My wife is not my wife."

He realizes he has found his wife, but she is not his wife. He knows that he will get divorced, even though he's barely married. He thinks it will take some time.

He hopes Alice will wait for him. And one day, perhaps she will say yes.

He only has one letter to convince her that he is not completely mad. So, struck by a flash of inspiration, he finds a pen and a scrap of paper in his pocket and begins to write, throwing down ideas in no particular order, but it doesn't matter because he will write this letter over and over again, for days and nights. But where should he send it? To which address? He doesn't know where she lives, goes out, goes, or ... perhaps ... a bench in the Jardin du Luxembourg, on the right-hand side, opposite the pond with the toy boats, the same place he met her by chance the previous day.

14.
Paris, 8 May 1955

"May I, *mademoiselle*?"

Jules indicates the space on the bench next to the young woman who is sitting there upright, with a serious air about her and one hand on a book, as she stares into the distance.

She turns round to look at him. He is handsome with his brown hair, brushed back with brilliantine. His smile lights up his thin, angular face and his blue eyes that express both gravity and joy, depth and frivolity.

"Of course, please do."

They are in the Jardin du Luxembourg, a place she likes to come, always to the same spot, on the right when you look at the pond, beside the rows of green chairs. Slightly discolored and stained by storms, they bear the effects of time, like the flowers that come back to life again in spring, the trees, horse chestnuts, orange trees, Atlas cedars, Judas trees, huge hedges, thujas, sequoias, ginkgo, and elms, and like children that grow, that inhabit the garden, and brighten it up with their cries that mingle with the birdsong, and all the men and women who come and sit here, love each other here, for a season, or for a lifetime.

Her long hair falls over her shoulders, caught by the breeze, and caresses her face. Her light cotton skirt and her beige woolen twin-set highlight her slim, elegant, graceful figure. Fragile, nimble, aloof, she looks like she is going to soar up into the sky. He nods slightly by way of a greeting and gets distracted as he looks at her red lips, thin nose, melancholy gaze, and small, plump, still childlike hands.

She smiles back. She looks straight ahead again, concentrating. Her young face is expressive; she observes him like she's on the lookout.

She left home alone, walked up Rue Lhomond, down Rue d'Ulm to the Pantheon, then took the grand Rue Soufflot to get to the Jardin du Luxembourg. She sat down on her favorite bench to rest and dream in front of the pond where the small sailboats launched by children drift. This is where she cat-naps, reflects, and slips into her memories. When she was a child, she used to come to this garden with her parents. She played with stones for hours on end. One afternoon, she had choked on a stone she had swallowed; her father had held her upright and squeezed her chest to make her spit it out. He had saved her that day, but it had left her with a fear of swallowing when she ate stringy food or swallowed tablets.

She looks up and, with a certain amount of curiosity, observes the man who has sat down beside her. He's dressed elegantly in a V-neck sweater over a white shirt and beige chinos—bright, understated colors for this May morning.

Sitting beside each other, they hold themselves gracefully, move with ease, and are filled with suppressed desires; they seem lost in another world, smiling.

He turns toward her and looks at her with sadness and resignation. She looks at him, her face frozen in an undefinable expression, somewhere between doubt and disbelief. What is he doing in the garden at this time of day when people are working? He is reading history at the Sorbonne. Later, he would like to become a museum director or an archaeologist. He likes the idea of investigating origins and discovering forgotten civilizations.

Archaeologist, a wonderful profession. Which region? Which period is he interested in? Does he know Egypt? Has he heard about the discovery of the Dead Sea Scrolls? She has just matriculated in the Arts Faculty. She would like to teach in a high school. Hosted by a children's home, she had lived with other children for a time. She likes playing with them, dressing up to entertain them, and telling them stories. When she's with adults, she feels out of place.

"You miss your childhood," he notes.

She looks at him, suddenly taken aback.

"This bench is where my parents sat while I played. That's why I like coming to the Jardin du Luxembourg."

A gentle breeze rustles the majestic, exotic trees and the enormous sequoias above them, like a canopy offering centennial shade. A ray of sunlight pierces the foliage. The air is sweet; it almost feels like you're in the countryside.

She runs her hand through her hair to tame it. She looks at him and listens to the story he is telling in a calm, deep voice without taking his eyes off her.

He tells her about May 8th. He was only a child when the sirens and church bells rang out. Everyone had gone down into the streets to hear General De Gaulle announce the Allied victory via loudspeaker. In the yellow photos, he poses with his brother in a village in the middle of Isère. He becomes emotional when he talks about his mother and the bread she used to make. Every Friday, her hands would endlessly knead the dough—this memory chokes his heart, and he holds back his tears. Why did she stay in the house when their father had taken them, him and his brother, for a walk in the mountains? Why hadn't she gone with them that day?

"It's strange," he says. "I don't know why I'm telling you all this. I've never talked to anyone about it."

"Since the war, it feels like I'm living in a constant void."

"How old are you?"

"Eighteen," she says. "And you?"

"Twenty-two. I'm not much older than you."

"We're adults, and we haven't started to live yet."

All of a sudden, he looks at her.

"May I?"

She smiles at him, and he dares to take her hand gently. He feels the warmth of her delicate skin, which he caresses for a moment before briefly bringing it to his mouth.

"I'm Jules," he says. "Jules Gardot."

"Nice to meet you, Jules."

"Where do you live?"

And that is how it happened, at first sight. And the fear of losing her was already there. Where do you live? As though it was the most important question in the world. *Somewhere, on planet Earth. Under the heavenly sky is where I live, where it is always dark. Apart from this very moment when a flash has lit up the sky. Under the stars, the ones that are currently above us, even though it is the middle of the day, have you noticed? Just like this shooting star whose light streaks the sky, simply through the sparkle in your eyes. Since you looked at me, I no longer know where I live. I don't have a name, I don't remember anything, nothing but your interest in me. I would live anywhere with you if that was what you so desired. But what does this question mean: Where do you live? And how should I know now that I have met you? I can no longer find that mysterious place where I had taken refuge, where I lived without existing, where I was hiding to protect myself so that I would not have to suffer humankind.*

"*Adieu, mademoiselle,*" Jules says. "It was a pleasure to meet you."

Then, unsettled, he gets up, gives a brief nod, and slowly leaves, uncertain of his step.

She watches him as he walks away, down the long path, toward the entrance.

"See you again soon, Jules," she murmurs.

Mademoiselle,

When you left in a rush yesterday, without leaving a trace, I forgot to tell you one thing: We shall spend the next sixty years together.

We shall get married in Cabourg, in that nice hotel that looks out over the sea. Your deep, sorrowful eyes will gaze into mine, and you will shed tears like a child. And when I look at you, I shall forget everything—the past that has damaged us, this terrible world we have been left with. I shall take care of you and heal your wounds. We shall go on our honeymoon to Naples and Capri, and under a starry sky, I shall swear an oath to you, and my love. I shall watch you wander along the banks of the Seine in Paris, in all seasons, at all stages of our lives, and in my heart, in the most delicate part, on which you trampled last night by not saying goodbye. When you dig your fingers into my arm, I will know that you are giving birth. It will be a tiny little girl who will have your eyes and my expression. And your incredible ability to look at creatures and things with an insatiable curiosity. I will feel, in seeing your tears, that there is something greater than us, and I will not be able to do anything for you other than renew this promise of love, a love that lasts.

I know we shall go through trials, with highs and lows, commitments made and broken, the tribulations of life, moments of doubt, and betrayals. I know I will no longer kiss you; you shall feel transparent before me when all I see is you. We shall fight, and, worse still, we shall bicker like cat and dog. You will want to leave me, and you will want to stay. You will have weighed it up long and hard and decided against it; you will have prepared everything. Do not say no, even though you will never admit it to me. I would have done the same thing in your place; perhaps I would even have had the courage to leave that day. I would have behaved like a son of a bitch, you will have told me a thousand times; sometimes we'll be foolish, trying to prove we are the strongest. But I beg you, Alice, may I call you Alice, I really want you to stay on the day you have packed your bags to leave. I promise I'll be tidy. I promise not to get water all over the bathroom when I get washed. And I won't wake you up too early in the morning; I know that you sometimes suffer from insomnia. These are little things, but they will all make our lives easier . . .

You will still hesitate, you will leave, you will come back. And we will still be together when our friends are no longer our friends, when our parents have passed away, when our children have left to lead their own lives. We will finish this life together, in a house by the sea. In the evening, when it's dark, I will fall asleep in your arms. Perhaps our memories will fail us. Perhaps we will lose our sight, our hearing, and our hair. Perhaps we will develop dementia. Illness and old age will prevent us from recognizing ourselves. You will be extremely patient. Not like me, Alice. May I call you darling? We shall be so united that we shall be one. I must see you again, very soon, to explain everything to you. It will take a long time. I will start writing my story from the end, at the time we shall meet again on this bench, and we shall no lon-

ger recognize each other because we will have lost our mem-
ories. We will have experienced everything and forgotten ev-
erything that binds us, even the existence of our children, our
wedding in Cabourg, our honeymoon to Naples and Capri,
birthdays, marriages, and deaths. We shall be like strangers,
one with the other, no longer knowing that we once loved
each other. Do not be sad. We shall be ready to love each
other again. It shall be like the first time we met.

Alice, may I sit here beside you? Will you come and meet
me on this bench tomorrow? I am already waiting there for
you and for life, this life that I can no longer imagine without
you.

Yours, Jules

Also available from Éliette Abécassis

If Only
ISBN 978-1-64690-038-1
Grand Books
Available now

Amélie and Vincent meet as students at the Sorbonne at the end of the 1980s. It's love at first sight for both, but neither dares confess their feelings to the other. They agree to meet again, but Amélie is late. And in those few minutes, it's not just a date she misses out on, but her entire life.

Vincent and Amélie get swept up by life as it carries them toward fates they no longer control, jobs they didn't choose, marriages and relationships that become rocky. Life that takes them down paths, through doors, into hallways, for ten, twenty, or thirty years . . .

It is the story of two lives in parallel across the decades, the story of their relationships and careers, the story of chance encounters that bring them together again and again. Will chance give them the opportunity to get together?